FIC
PAU

Paul, Barba

Good King
Sauerkraut

$16.95

DATE		
DEC 1 1989		
DEC 2 5 1989		
JAN 10 01		

WITHDRAWN

New Florence Community Library
BOX 248
NEW FLORENCE, PA. 15944
© THE BAKER & TAYLOR CO.

GOOD KING SAUERKRAUT

By the same author

He Huffed and He Puffed
But He Was Already Dead When I Got There
Kill Fee
The Renewable Virgin

GOOD KING SAUERKRAUT

Barbara Paul

Charles Scribner's Sons
New York

Copyright © 1989 by Barbara Paul

All rights reserved. No part of this book may be reproduced or transmitted in any form or by any means, electronic or mechanical, including photocopying, recording, or by any information storage and retrieval system, without permission in writing from the Publisher.

Charles Scribner's Sons
Macmillan Publishing Company
866 Third Avenue, New York, NY 10022
Collier Macmillan Canada, Inc.

This is a work of fiction. Names, characters, places, and incidents either are the product of the author's imagination or are used fictitiously. Any resemblance to actual events or persons, living or dead, is entirely coincidental.

Library of Congress Cataloging-in-Publication Data
Paul, Barbara, 1931–
  Good King Sauerkraut/Barbara Paul.
    p. cm.
  ISBN 0-684-19089-3
  I. Title.
  PS3566.A82615G66 1989
  813'.54—dc20   89-6179   CIP

10 9 8 7 6 5 4 3 2 1
Printed in the United States of America

GOOD KING SAUERKRAUT

* 1 *

A long metal arm reached out, touched the front panel of the black box, and identified the box as a safe. One of the mechanical hand's two fingers pressed against the surface near the dial and "read" the safe's combination. The two fingers locked themselves into the form of a gripper, turned the dial to the right numbers, and swung the safe door open. So far so good.

The hand reached into the safe and set about the business of identifying the first of three objects that had been placed there. On a computer screen thirty feet away a thermal image began to build up of a block of wood with a number of nails driven in flush with the surface; the robot's memory came up with the words to make the identification complete. The second item took a little longer, but the robot was able to record the presence of a batch of papers held together by two paper clips, one made of plastic and the other of metal. The manipulating fingers even counted the pages. It was the third object that caused trouble.

It was an ordinary stoppered test tube. The sensors were able to differentiate between the glass tube and the rubber stopper but couldn't recognize that particular combination of materials and shapes. The robot had been programmed to bring back any object it couldn't identify, so the gripper fingers picked up the test tube—and promptly crushed it.

The two human beings in the room looked at each other and sighed. "See what it does next," the woman said.

The robot ran through its program options and chose one. A panel opened in the machine's squat body and a second arm appeared, one that was limited to self-maintenance work. It disconnected the gripper that had crushed the test tube and attached a much smaller one, one designed for work more delicate than swinging open safe doors.

"A little late for that," the man growled. "Why didn't the sensors tell it a smaller gripper was called for?"

"Dunno. They should have."

Almost daintily the small gripper picked up the largest glass fragments and deposited them in a carry box positioned where the robot's head would have been if it had had one. Bearing its prize of broken glass, the machine rolled back to where the man and woman sat at the control board.

Gale Fredericks typed in a test command on the keyboard. "It looked to me as if it simply overestimated the distance between its fingers and the test tube . . . no, that's not it. The ultrasonic proximity sensor system checks out. The infrared sensors in the fingertips are okay."

"The gripper just squeezed too hard. Check the force transducers."

She did. "They're all right too. But 'test tube' isn't in the robot's vocabulary."

"That shouldn't make any difference. Whether it knows what a test tube is or not, it should have been able to determine it was a container of some sort. 'A container made of glass plus a rubber plug'—that's the conclusion it should have come to."

"Well, it's a software problem," Gale said. "Don't scowl so, King. Your sensors did their job."

"Maybe." If the robot had been given eyes, it would have recognized the test tube immediately. Tactile sensors, however, still had a way to go. King unfolded his bony frame from the chair on which he'd been slouching. When he stood up straight, which he never did, he was close to seven feet tall; every new person he met asked if he played basketball. "We did test the mechanical parts, didn't we?" He stepped over to the robot and began moving the arm up and down, back and forth.

"About an hour ago," Gale smiled. She repeated that it had to be a software problem and started speculating as to what might have gone wrong.

Only half listening, King examined the wrist connections of the robot's arm; he could see nothing wrong. Maybe the shoulder? He tried swinging the arm in an arc.

And almost hit Gale in the face. "Watch it!" she cried, jumping back in time. "For god's sake, King, pay attention!"

"Oh—sorry! I didn't hit you, did I? Uh, next time cough or something?"

She gave an exasperated laugh. "I was *talking* to you!"

He tried not to look sheepish. Lowering his voice, he spoke as authoritatively as he knew how: "All right, Gale, let's get on it. I want to know why the grippers weren't changed in time as well as—"

"Right," she smiled. "First thing Monday morning."

"Monday?"

"Look at the time! Work week is over—everybody else has gone home." Sure enough, the lab was empty except for the two of them, something King had failed to notice. "Besides," Gale added, "Bill wants to go a ball game. The Pirates could move into first place tonight."

Husbands, King thought gloomily. They were even worse than wives. "Might as well shut down, then."

"I'll take care of it. I have to go to the rest room first, though." She was halfway out the door before she thought to say, "Oh—you want to come to the game with us?"

"No," he said, and remembered to add, "thank you."

She'd barely left when the phone rang. "King? Bill Fredericks. Is Gale available?"

"She's in the Ladies'. Want to call back?"

"No, just tell her I'll be a few minutes late picking her up. You're about finished there, aren't you?"

King testily assured him they were indeed finished and he'd pass on the message. He'd forgotten about the call even before the receiver was back in the cradle. Gale was right; the problem had to be in the software. Tracking it down could take five minutes or five days. He decided to let Gale do the job. On Monday.

She came back in and saw him hovering over the board. "You're not going to work on this any more today, are you? Shall I shut down?"

"Yes, go ahead."

Gale moved quickly around the cluttered, barn-sized laboratory room, disconnecting the various robot parts they'd been testing. There was no way to keep a neat lab while working with manipulators of all sizes and shapes, plus end-of-arm tooling and all the hardware necessary to make the various parts work. Keystone Robotics was perhaps a little messier than most, because King had a tendency to leave things wherever he happened to be when he finished using them. "Don't start on the software," she told him. "I'll get to it Monday."

"All right," he answered vaguely, his mind still on the crushed test tube.

"Well . . . good night, King."

"G'night." Gale left, for her husband and a baseball game. After the two years she'd been working there, King was still naively surprised when she preferred to go home to Bill instead of staying and working with him.

King slouched down at his computer terminal and stared at the screen, feeling a tad sorry for himself. They were trying to come up with something even more versatile than the electrically conductive gripping pads developed at the Georgia Tech Research Institute, but to date they hadn't had a perfect test yet, not one. The robot should have worked. Gale should have stayed. The week should have been longer.

Should, should, should; there were altogether too many *shoulds* in his life. Always had been. His full name was King Sarcowicz, and he earnestly wished it weren't. The Sarcowicz wasn't so bad; it was just another of those names that always have to be spelled out for mail-order clerks and airline reservation agents. It was the King part that gave him trouble; it had made his childhood somewhat less than idyllic and plagued him still in middle age.

King's mother had firmly believed that a child lived up to or down to his name. Any boy unlucky enough to be named Elbert, for example, couldn't help but be a jerk. Cosmo would be a gangster, Clark a newspaper reporter, Bruno a professional wrestler, and Percy a . . . well. So she'd named her only offspring King, unknowingly setting an unrealizable standard for a boy who was by nature about as regal as Carl "Alfalfa" Switzer. As long as she had this thing for royalty, King often wondered, why couldn't she have named him Earl? A grand name, Earl. Or even Duke would have done, although he might have had trouble with the two-fisted John Wayneness of that one. But anything would have been better than King.

"Not a very kingly thing to do," his mother would say whenever he'd done something dumb, accompanying the pronouncement with a sad little shake of her head. It was her favorite reprimand. By the time he'd reached twenty she had more or less given up on him and stopped saying it, but the headshake remained. Then just five years ago, shortly after King's fortieth birthday, his mother had passed away, still shaking her head. Even now when he did something especially stupid, he could hear her voice in his ear: *Not a very kingly thing to do.*

Not that she'd actually been ashamed of him, of his awkwardness and his inability to shine in company; it was simply that she didn't go out of her way to introduce him to the friends and neighbors of her later years. She'd been pleased no end when King bought her a house in Allentown, just far enough away from Pittsburgh to make frequent visits inconvenient—an arrangement that suited them both very well. She knew he made a lot of money, although at times she'd wondered whether it might not all be a big mistake somebody was making. Somebody who? "I'm my own boss now, Ma," he'd tell her and watch as she smiled uncertainly and shook her head.

King shook his own head; it seemed the only times he thought of his mother any more were those increasingly frequent moments when his control over his own domain got a bit precarious. Like when robots failed tests. Like when seemingly foolproof software programs didn't work. Like when Gale Fredericks thought it more important to go to an idiotic baseball game with sweet old Bill than stay at the lab and find out what had gone wrong.

But King hadn't objected (out loud), nor would he raise the subject in the future. No, by golly, he was going to be an "understanding" employer, he was. Most of the Keystone technicians didn't like working with him, the dorks; they complained he expected them to read his mind. But Gale had been able to keep up with him, and King was being very careful to do nothing to alienate her. Besides, she was one of the few people he knew whom he genuinely liked. King had a way of making . . . not enemies, exactly, but antagonists, he guessed you could call them, and without even meaning to. It was a state of affairs King found totally unfathomable. But unfathomable or not, there it was: he had to tiptoe around people whose good will he wanted to keep.

He stared at a design on his computer screen that he'd been working on earlier in the day, a design for a system to retract sensing fingers inside larger ones so the gripper-changing function of the robot's self-maintenance arm could be done away with. He could see more problems than the thing was probably worth, and if he started on them now he'd be there all night. He reached out a hand to save the program and knocked over a Styrofoam cup that, naturally, still had coffee in it. The brown liquid spread quickly over a pile of unopened mail; King looked around for one of the rolls of paper towels that were always kept handy and started dabbing irritably at the mess. *Not a very kingly thing to do.*

He ended up spreading the mail out to dry and in the process found a set of demonstration disks for a new CAD program. The disks, fortunately, were in a sealed plastic container and had been untouched by the deluge. King was just slipping the first disk into the computer to try it out when the phone rang again.

It was his partner, Dennis Cox. "Big doin's, King. How close are you to a stopping point?"

"I'm stopped now."

"Good. Come on over." The phone went dead.

King scowled at the receiver. "Lawsy, I have been *summoned,*" he said aloud to the empty laboratory. Dennis claimed he couldn't think in the midst of the clutter of King's lab, so all their meetings had to take place in his office. King resented that. He even resented the resentment; it was a schoolboy reaction to what was nothing more than petty bullying. Game-playing.

But that was what Dennis did best, play games. He'd started in the day they first opened the doors of Keystone Robotics, back when there were three partners instead of just two. The exigencies of the first year of operation had proved too much for partner number three, who quickly began to yearn for the comforting security of a steady paycheck. So when Westinghouse eventually crooked its corporate finger at all three of them, the third partner had gone a-runnin'. If he'd stayed, he'd have been a moderately wealthy man by now, or at least conspicuously upscale. But it was just as well he'd gone, King thought; he hadn't much liked the guy anyway.

So now there were just King Sarcowicz and Dennis Cox, both of them designers of things robotic but with King thinking up most of their new technology while Dennis eased more and more into management. And management had just summoned technology to its office.

King opened the office door without knocking and walked in. "What couldn't wait until Monday?"

Dennis Cox was a good-looking man when he wasn't angry—blue-eyed, blond, and ostentatiously tanned the year round. And he was anything but angry now; he gave King his best cat-swallowed-the-canary smile. "Wait 'til you hear. I've had a call from Warren Osterman at MechoTech in New York. He just got back from Washington . . . with a pocketful of new DARPA contracts."

King inhaled sharply. "Well? Do we get the subcontract?"

"Didn't you feel the earth shake? We got it! And from the clues Osterman dropped, I'd say the budget is *ee*-normous." King let out a whoop. Dennis went on, "He wants us to come to New York next week. All that time I spent sucking up to the old fart finally paid off."

DARPA contracts weren't exactly the lifeblood of the robotics industry, but they did mean serious money. A great deal of what was new in technology was the direct result of experiments funded by the Defense Advanced Research Projects Agency, headquartered in the Defense Sciences Office in Arlington; DARPA was always on the lookout for new military applications. "Which project do we get?"

"He wouldn't say over the phone. But what does it matter? Any one of 'em will put us over the top."

King knew that; it was what they'd been waiting for. The new contracts were for the much-desired, long-awaited automated battlefield. He and Dennis had been consulted time and again by both MechoTech and Washington; the talk was always of various possible robot-controlled superweapons that the Defense Department was itching to get its hands on. MechoTech had been talking not just to Keystone Robotics but to other outfits as well, preparing whatever presentation had eventually convinced DARPA that MechoTech was just the company to raise the mechanizing of warfare to a high art. "The government's been working on the automated battlefield for years," King mused. "Why are we just now getting in on it?"

"High failure rate. Ruh-ho-botics is the latest to take a header, I'm happy to say." Dennis was making fun of a rival firm called Rhobotics International, which had underbid Keystone on a couple of past occasions. "Warren Osterman says if we can manage the project he's going to give us, there'll be more work than we can handle until the year 3000."

The two partners grinned at each other. This was the project that could make them the standard-setters, the ones who determined what "state of the art" meant. The good news made each of them feel more friendly toward the other than either had felt in years. On impulse King stuck out his hand; Dennis laughed and shook it.

"And we don't have to bid on it?" King asked.

"Nope. It's all settled—MechoTech says it's ours. But now the bad news." He paused, making King wait for it. "Osterman wants those two yups from Silicon Valley on the project with us."

"Which two yups?"

Dennis took a deep breath. "Gregory Dillard and Mimi Hargrove."

"Oh, *shit!*" King dragged up a chair and sat down, not noticing Dennis wince when he banged the chair against the desk. "Why those two, for god's sake?"

"Osterman says they write better programs than we do. Look, King, I know you and Mimi don't get along. But on a project this big, you can make the effort not to strangle her, can't you? She and Gregory always work as a team, you know—we've got to take them both."

King didn't mention that Gregory Dillard had even more reason to stick knives in him than Mimi Hargrove did. "Sure, I can make the effort. But will she?"

"Of course she will. She'd put up with the devil himself to get in on this deal."

"Thanks a lot."

"Ah, you know what I mean. Besides, we've been having more software problems than usual lately, haven't we?"

King glared at him suspiciously. "You've been pumping Gale Fredericks for information."

Dennis looked astonished. "I've been reading your goddam *reports*, King! You were the one who insisted we keep each other informed, for crying out loud."

King didn't remember it that way but let it pass. "We can solve the software problems," he insisted stubbornly. "We've got good programmers."

"You're not listening. Warren Osterman has already decided. Mimi and Gregory are part of the package."

King's skin started itching, a sure sign of people trouble. Hardware trouble he could handle, and even software trouble, given time. But certain people, an embarrassingly large number of certain people, always left him with his nerve ends exposed. Mimi Hargrove and he had locked horns the first time they'd met, at an international robotics congress . . . and things had stayed downside ever since.

King and Dennis talked a while longer, speculating as to which part of the Defense Department's grand vision of a totally automated battlefield MechoTech was subcontracting to them. Dennis indulged in a little bragging about his contacts in the bigger firm, but King was convinced it was his own work with tactile sensors that had brought Keystone in on the project. By tacit agreement they avoided the subject of the pair from Silicon Valley; they'd had to work with incompatible people before and they could do it again.

Dennis looked at his watch. "I have a date tonight and I need to soak in the tub a while first—my back's killing me. Osterman wants us in New York on Wednesday. Will two days be enough to get Gale set up to handle things while you're away?"

"Should be."

"Good. We'll take the eight o'clock flight Wednesday morning, then."

Business concluded, the two partners went their separate ways—Dennis to a night on the town with the latest of the chorus of great-looking women he'd accumulated since his divorce (where did he find them?), and King to . . . ? He climbed into the aging Buick Dennis had told him repeatedly to get rid of. His oniomaniac partner drove a Mercedes 560 SL with a license plate that made King shudder: ROBOT-1. But buying a new car was a lot of effort, and King kept putting it off. The Buick still got him to where he needed to go.

His route home took him through Squirrel Hill, where he stopped at Rhoda's Deli to pick up three dozen eggs and a six-pack of Heineken. King lived in the Shadyside section of Pittsburgh, in a house designed for a large family but which suited King and his clutter very well. Unfortunately, the big house was a lot smaller now than when he'd first moved in; it seemed to shrink a little more each year. As he pulled into the driveway he saw Mrs. Rowe next door peeking out through the curtains. When he looked at her, she pulled back from the window.

King turned off the engine and sat thinking. Now what had he forgotten to do? Mrs. Rowe didn't like to complain when he'd neglected something. She just peeked at him through the curtains; that had come to be his signal. He took his eggs and beer and got out of the car to look around.

Ah. The garbage cans.

Mrs. Rowe was eighty and arthritic; King helped her out with things she couldn't manage on her own whenever he could. He was pretty good about remembering to carry her garbage cans to the curb for collection, but he didn't always remember to bring them back in. Yesterday had been collection day; that meant he'd driven past the empty cans at least three times without seeing them. He hurried to haul them in along with his own. Old Mrs. Rowe had probably been worrying about those cans all day.

A yellow Post-it note was stuck to his front door, written in a round schoolgirlish hand:

Dear Mr. Sarkowiz,
 You forgot to leave the check again. Please remember to mail it tomorrow.

Sincerely yours,
Ready-Maid Cleaning Service

King was annoyed—not because they'd misspelled his name (everybody did that), but because they'd left the note out where anyone could see it. But his annoyance evaporated once he'd gone inside. King liked coming home to an empty house. He had enough of people yammering at him all day and demanding immediate decisions and instant solutions and delivery by last Tuesday; the welcoming silence of his home was a great soother-of-jitters. For a time he'd had a cat that met him at the door every night; but King had forgotten to feed him just once too often and the animal deserted him for Mrs. Rowe next door. This embarrassed the old lady. But the cat was still there; King caught a glimpse of him every once in a while.

He opened a beer and scrambled six of the eggs for supper. While he ate he thought about automated mobile weapons and intelligence-gathering devices. Remote piloted vehicles that could go into the field and send back information to a central computer. Mine-planters. Detectors that read seismic disturbances in the ground to deduce number and direction of troop movements. Small, inconspicuous bombs that could drive themselves to a specified target area and then set themselves off. "Smart" bullets. Self-repairing fully automatic tanks, boldly going where no tank has gone before. Battles fought by machines, remote-controlled war.

The idea of a totally automated battlefield had been lovingly nourished by various government agencies for the past thirty years, but of late most of the attention (and money) had gone to missile development. Killing from a safe distance, like David and his slingshot. But when the Strategic Defense Initiative boys had announced their sheltering umbrella would have a few holes in it, that the Star Wars defense could protect only military installations and not cities—then the automated battlefield was suddenly everybody's favorite baby again. The budget, as Dennis Cox had said, must be *ee*-normous. And MechoTech had been handed a major hunk of it.

MechoTech did some design work of its own, but primarily it was a manufacturer that drew upon whatever innovations it could acquire the patents for. Keystone Robotics had dealt with MechoTech before; its president, Warren Osterman, knew their work and was pleased with it. King didn't know Osterman well, but the MechoTech president seemed to be one of those people who always knew things that other people only read about in the papers weeks later. King tended to respect his judgment, and the fact that Osterman had handpicked Mimi Hargrove and Gregory Dillard to design the software on this new project, whatever it was, made him pause. It was only a few years ago that Mimi and Gregory and three others had broken away from Ashton-Tate Corporation to found SmartSoft in Santa Clara, where they'd quickly established themselves as leaders in the field of robot programming. There was no question that they were good, but King was more than content to have the width of the continent between them and Keystone; why look for trouble?

The first time King ever saw Mimi Hargrove had been in Berlin, a little over six years earlier; that was before she'd teamed up with Gregory Dillard. The occasion was a biannual congress for the exchange of ideas among people who worked in robotics, and Mimi had been delivering a paper about software problems connected with surgical robots. King had spotted what he was sure was a logic flaw in one of her algorithms and had stood up in that packed auditorium to say so. He'd gone on to question a few other things, to which she'd had no immediate answers. Then he'd innocently suggested she test her theories before presenting them and sat down, not realizing he'd offered her the ultimate insult before her fellow professionals. The session eventually ended and the audience started drifting out.

It wasn't until someone stopped by King's seat and asked why he'd "attacked" Mimi that it occurred to him he might have been out of line. To him it was purely an intellectual problem and personalities shouldn't be allowed to enter into it; getting the machines to work right was the important thing, wasn't it?

Dennis Cox, groaning softly in the next seat, had explained it to him. "You remember that scene in *Amadeus* when Mozart takes a simple little tune that Salieri wrote and turns it into something grand? He goes merrily improvising along, totally oblivious to the feelings of the man he's showing up as inferior. Well, you just did something like that to Mimi Hargrove."

"Good god—I didn't mean that!"

" 'Mean'," Dennis had said wryly, "doesn't count. You're careless with people, King. You humiliated her. You asked her to prove things she couldn't prove without putting in hours at a computer with all of us watching over her shoulder. And then you implied she wasn't even professional enough to test out her solutions before offering them."

King's skin had started itching, nervously. "Do you think I should apologize?"

"I think you should try."

King had stood up immediately and apologized, but by then most of the audience had dispersed. Mimi was eventually able to publish papers supporting the points King had questioned and thus restore her reputation, which wasn't all that badly damaged to begin with. But she never forgave him for insinuating publicly that she didn't know what she was doing, and every meeting of the two since then had been tense and uncomfortable. King had heard via the grapevine that Mimi had let it be known she would never ever under any circumstances whatsoever at any time or in any place work with Keystone Robotics.

Yet there she was out in California getting ready to do just that. Did that mean she'd forgiven him? King wasn't naive enough to think that; it was more likely she had something up her sleeve. Something like humiliating him the way he'd humiliated her.

King cleared off the table and put his dishes in the dishwasher, absentmindedly including the empty beer bottle along with them. Mimi must want this project pretty badly to consent to work with him. And that must mean she knew more about it than he and Dennis Cox did. Or more than Dennis had told him. Dennis held things back sometimes; he liked knowing more than his partner.

People not telling people what they know—it was only then that King remembered he hadn't told Gale Fredericks her husband would be late picking her up. Oh well, they'd get together eventually and go on to their ball game. Bill Fredericks would drive up Hi-Honey-what's-wrong and Gale would yell at him for being late. He would protest he'd left a message with her boss, and she'd say he should know better than to count on King to remember. Bill would snarl something and Gale would snap back at him, and they'd end up arguing through the entire ball game before they finally made up and decided it was all King Sarcowicz's fault.

Whew. That little fantasy didn't turn out too well.

Besides, he'd never once heard Gale raise her voice in anger; maybe he secretly wanted her to fight with her husband. *I'm not a goddam message center,* King thought testily and decided to put it to rest for a while. He needed some distraction before going to bed; otherwise he'd lie there for hours worrying about Gale Fredericks and Dennis Cox and Mimi Hargrove and the MechoTech project.

After a moment's thought he slipped *Aliens* into the VCR. He opened another beer and settled down to watch the marvelous mechanical monsters do their thing.

* 2 *

The next morning King poached four eggs for breakfast and hardboiled six others to take with him. He waved goodbye to Mrs. Rowe, who started every other day by sweeping off her front walk, and drove away. Keystone Robotics was closed on Saturdays; occasionally a technician or a manager would come in to finish a job, but usually King had the place to himself.

After he'd checked in with security, the first thing King saw in the lab was his computer screen glowing away; he'd forgotten to shut down. Yesterday he'd been about to try a new computer-aided design program when Dennis Cox had imperiously summoned him to his office, forgetting which of them was named King—and the new CAD program had been forgotten. King cleared the screen, relieved to see the image had left no afterburn. But as long as the program was already loaded . . .

Three-quarters of an hour later he unloaded the new CAD in annoyance; it was one of those programs that redrew the screen every time the user panned or changed views, making the whole design process a lot slower than King liked. Computer-aided delay. For a three-thousand-dollar price tag, they were going to have to do better than that. He put the package aside for Gale Fredericks to look at later.

Saturday was King's reward for putting up with Monday through Friday. Once a week he put Keystone's contracted projects aside and played with whatever designs struck his fancy. Every now and then one of them panned out and Keystone was able to make money out of it; but the real purpose of Saturdays was to allow King to experiment without any specific end in view and without a deadline hanging over his head. And with the advent of desktop manufacturing, King could see the results of his experimenting sooner and a lot more cheaply than before. The computer used a laser and powdered plastic or metal to create prototypes of robot parts, and it did it in a matter of hours instead of the weeks and even months the traditional manufacturing methods took.

King called up a design for a driverless vehicle he'd been doodling with for several Saturdays. The problem was finding a method of obstacle avoidance without having to plant sensors along the road to guide the vehicle. King had vaguely had public transportation in mind when he'd started the design; but with the new DARPA contract constantly hovering at the edge of his attention, he saw no reason the vehicle couldn't be adapted to troop transport. He got to work.

He worked steadily until about one o'clock when he looked up to see Dennis Cox picking his way with exaggerated caution through the laboratory's obstacle course. *Now what's he up to?* King thought with resignation. The only time Dennis came to the lab was when he wanted to talk King into something. King saved the program he was working on and waited, hands clasped loosely in his lap.

Dennis pulled up a chair and eased himself down on it carefully. "Back's still bothering me," he complained. "Look, King, there's something we'd better settle before we go to New York. Right now it looks like a four-person team, but MechoTech can still pull in somebody else. But even if it stays only you and me and Mimi Hargrove and Gregory Dillard, one of us is going to have to be in charge."

King's eyebrows shot up. "Me," he said, surprised that needed to be talked about.

Dennis licked his lips and spoke carefully. "No, King. Not you."

"What do you mean, not me? I'm the one who's going to be doing the primary design work. Everything will have to originate with me."

"Originate with you, yes. And you'll do a helluva job. You're one of the best designers I've ever seen, King."

First the stroke, King thought.

"But, alas and alack, you are one *lousy* organizer."

Then the poke.

"You forget deadlines," Dennis said, "you ignore paperwork, you don't remember to tell others what you're doing. You go off on some tangent of your own and then get mad when we can't read your mind and keep up with you. You alienate the people who work for you."

"Not everybody," King said defensively, thinking of Gale Fredericks.

"You really believe Mimi Hargrove will take orders from you?"

King was silent a moment and then said, "She'll have to, if I'm in charge and she wants to stay on the project. Dennis, I'm the only one who *can* run the project. Unless you're planning to do all the designing yourself?"

Dennis's face tightened; that barb struck home. "Warren Osterman doesn't know anything about your work habits, and he'll probably want to make you project leader . . . unless you tell him I'm a better manager than you are. Which I am. And you know it. What do you think Mimi Hargrove and Gregory Dillard are doing out in California right now? They're tossing a coin to see which one of *them* is going to be in charge."

"A software person? That's ridiculous," King scoffed, unconvincingly.

Dennis shook his head. "Not so ridiculous. Gregory Dillard was put in charge of a submersible project the Navy contracted to Rhobotics International two years ago. Gregory convinced the Navy that software people were needed to head it up to keep the 'boy geniuses' from going overboard. He meant the designers. Now if he got away with that once, you know damn well he's going to try it again. He'll either back Mimi or she'll back him, you can count on it."

"Hell."

"So they're going to go into MechoTech next Wednesday with it all worked out which one of them should run the project. And if we want to keep control ourselves, we're going to have to do the same thing. Then it'll just be a matter of persuading Warren Osterman."

King's stomach rumbled. He got up and started wandering around the lab while Dennis continued his pitch. His partner was right on both counts; Dennis was the better organizer, and those two in California undoubtedly were conspiring to take over the project. It was the one thing King hated about his business—the politicking. Of necessity all their projects were big ones; robotics work did not come cheap. It seemed obvious to him that the one who thought up the robot and made it work had to be the one in charge, so obvious that any challenge to that Universal Truth left him frustrated and helpless.

There was something else, too. Dennis didn't know, but Gregory Dillard would be even more unhappy about taking orders from King than Mimi Hargrove would. The year before, King had run into Gregory quite by accident, in San Francisco, at one of the exhibitions of new high-tech products that were being held throughout the country with increasing frequency. Gregory and his wife Karen were looking at a housekeeping robot; after an exchange of amenities, all three of them watched a demonstration.

One of the robot's design team conducted the demonstration, a man named Johnson or Thompson or something forgettable like that. The robot was a prototype, the man said, with bugs still to be worked out. A group of eight or ten people watched, as the robot first scrubbed and then waxed a small tile floor, moving a chair and a table and then replacing them as needed. Also on the demonstration floor was a raised hutch, its doors open to reveal shelves filled with breakable glassware. The robot's sensors told it this particular piece of furniture couldn't be moved without damaging its contents, so it carefully and neatly scrubbed and waxed around the hutch's four legs.

"Square legs," Gregory Dillard pointed out.

Johnson or Thompson admitted that was one of the bugs still to be worked out. They hadn't yet found a way to program the machine to accommodate irregularly shaped furniture legs. Gregory introduced himself as one of the owners of SmartSoft and started speculating on possible programming approaches that might solve the problem. He suggested using a second robot, a smaller one, perhaps only a couple of inches in diameter. The small robot could clean around the table legs and in corners; then it could use sound sensors to listen for the big housekeeping robot and dump whatever dirt it had collected in the big robot's path. That was one possibility.

Gregory talked on easily, reducing the programming problem to the level of a game he enjoyed playing. He was Mr. Smooth in person, managing to imply that SmartSoft was the nearest thing to programming heaven to be found on earth and that he himself fit perfectly the programming ideal of deity. The designer was obviously intrigued and asked if he thought SmartSoft would be interested in taking on the problem.

King was thinking; the whole thing had a vaguely familiar ring to it. Something he had seen once before, at a demonstration very much like this one . . .

"Got it!" he cried, interrupting Gregory in midsentence. "Haig-Marcus Robots, last year. They were working on a machine to do individual paint jobs on previously installed items, like the molding of a window frame. They were having trouble making the robot follow the contours of the wood."

"Did they ever get it?" Johnson or Thompson asked.

"Yeah, they got it." King told him the name of the software company in Massachusetts that had solved the problem.

The designer thanked him effusively and King said quite honestly that he was happy to oblige. That was one of the purposes of these exhibitions, after all; you gave a little, you got a little back. Johnson or Thompson would remember him and return the favor as soon as he could. King was feeling rather pleased with himself until he saw Gregory Dillard staring at him in cold fury.

Only then did it hit him. He'd undercut Gregory; he'd taken a possible contract away from SmartSoft and given it to a rival company. And he'd done it not only before a small group of onlookers but in front of the man's wife as well.

Karen Dillard was tugging at her husband's sleeve and saying something quietly to him. Gregory allowed her to lead him away, but not before he'd moved over to King and hissed, "I won't forget this, you sonuvabitch."

Just remembering it made his skin itch. Dennis Cox would have handled it differently, and he'd even have enjoyed the chance to show off his moxie. Dennis would have waited until Gregory was out of earshot before passing on the information. Or, possibly, he would have said nothing at all to Johnson or Thompson and then let Gregory know he'd kept quiet, thus putting SmartSoft in his debt. Yes, that was more like Dennis. King of the manipulators, damn him.

"Well?" Dennis asked. "Have you been listening?"

"Of course I've been listening," King said hastily, wondering what he'd missed. If Dennis knew Gregory Dillard was gunning for him too, his partner would never give in. King's stomach growled again; he took a hardboiled egg out of his pocket and started peeling it. "I just don't agree with you, Dennis."

Dennis pointed his finger at him, annoying King even further; every time Dennis pointed his finger, his thumb stuck straight up in the air, making his hand look like a gun. "Remember one thing. United they win, divided we lose."

"Sure, no question there, we have to decide who's to run the project before we go to New York. What I'm not agreeing to is that it should be you."

"Jesus, King, you're just not plugged in at all, are you? Don't you understand? Mimi and Gregory aren't going to *let* you head the project."

King dropped a piece of eggshell on the floor, not noticing. "The last I heard, Warren Osterman was still in charge," he said tightly, wishing like hell that Dennis would drop the subject.

"But he'll base his decision on what he's told. And if those two tell him you're not qualified—and they will—he'll listen. They might, however, accept me as a viable compromise. But they sure as hell won't if *you* won't."

"The primary designer has got to be in charge," King insisted stubbornly. "It's my right."

"Oh, for Christ's sake, Sauerkraut, grow up!" Dennis snarled. "Here we are on the brink of losing control of the project and you're blathering on about your *rights*. For once in your life, do something practical!"

King turned rigid; that disparaging nickname *Sauerkraut* . . . it had a way of doing that to him, every time. "There's no point in going on with this," he said as coldly as he could. "Under no circumstances will I agree to work on a project that's run by the *secondary* designer."

It was Dennis's turn to stiffen. King's emergence as the more inventive designer of the two was not exactly a sore point between them—so long as King didn't rub it in. "Sleep on it," Dennis said, his face turning ugly with anger. "We'll talk again Monday." He got up and left, kicking a disembodied robot arm out of his way as he went.

King ate his hardboiled egg without tasting it and peeled another. He'd never asked Dennis where he'd picked up on that label "Sauerkraut"—it had been with King most of his life, and it looked as if he never was going to shake it. Goddammit. The nickname had first come into being when King was still a youngster, back when Walt Kelly's original *Pogo* was the most talked-about comic strip in the country. One of the ways Kelly had amused himself was by making up new words to familiar Christmas carols and having his denizens of the Okefenokee sing them once a year. One that Pogo and Churchy La Femme had warbled was *Good King Wenceslas*, which in Kelly's whimsical version had started out: "Good King Sauerkraut went out, on his feets uneven . . ."

On his feets uneven. What a dead perfect description of the young King Sarcowicz—stumbling, bumping into things, tripping over his own feet. The other kids had delighted in taunting him, calling him Good King Sauerkraut until he was sick to death of the sound of it. But after a time the first two words had disappeared, and it was just plain Sauerkraut from then on. The name dogged him everywhere; it had followed him to college and even on to work. Dennis Cox had never gone to school with King—they'd met when they were both doing some work for the Robotics Institute at Carnegie Mellon University—and yet Dennis had somehow learned of the loathsome soubriquet. That same thing had happened time and time again; it was a mystery King had never been able to solve.

Dennis never called him Sauerkraut out of mean-spiritedness, though; he saved it for those times when he was thoroughly angry. So now his partner was mad at him too, in company with Mimi Hargrove and Gregory Dillard. Oh, this was going to be one beaut of a project, it was. *Shit.*

But it was Dennis's own fault, King rationalized; he should have known King would never agree to pass the design responsibility over to him. They'd been in business only a couple of years when it became clear that Dennis Cox would never be anything more than a good journeyman designer. He was totally reliable in what he did, but the imagination and ingenuity that had made Keystone Robotics successful were all King's. Dennis had begun assuming the responsibilities of management as Keystone grew larger instead of hiring someone for the position, and he did a good job; he was needed in the office more than in the laboratory.

For the very first time, King contemplated the possibility that Dennis might resent that turn of affairs. His partner *seemed* quite happy making their money decisions for them, and god only knew King needed him to do it. Dennis did not go unappreciated by his partner. All in all, it was a symbiosis that King had pretty much assumed was as satisfactory to Dennis as it was to himself; but now he had to wonder if Dennis was indeed as comfortable in the role of secondary designer as he'd thought. If he weren't . . . King began to sweat. He didn't know what he'd do without Dennis.

But as worried as he was about getting the cooperation of the other three on the MechoTech project, he never once considered yielding control to one of them. It was unthinkable. Without King's designs, there was no project.

King put the problem out of his mind and worked steadily for four straight hours. When he finally shut down for the day, his neck and shoulders were stiff from sitting in the same position for so long. He reached high over his head and stretched his six feet ten inches until something popped; then he rotated his head and his arms. But the stiffness persisted, even during the drive home. Mrs. Rowe, he was happy to see, was not peeking out through her curtains.

He took a scalding hot shower, and that plus a beer eased the stiffness considerably. King didn't have much appetite, so dinner was two fried-egg sandwiches. Then he went into his study to perform his regular Saturday night chore of going through the week's mail.

But before he could get started, the doorbell rang. King groaned to himself when he saw the handsomely mustached, almost prissily dressed man on the other side of the now-opened door (too late!). Russ Panuccio, his closest friend. Whom he didn't like much. "Russ! What's up?"

Russ walked in uninvited. "Ginnie broke her leg. I just took her to Shadyside Hospital." Three blocks away. "You got any beer?"

"Yeah, sure. Is it a bad break?"

"Doctor says not. God, I hate hospitals."

King followed him into the kitchen, where Russ took a bottle of Heineken from the refrigerator. "How did it happen?"

"She fell down her front steps. I've been telling her for years those steps weren't safe. But you know Ginnie—lets things drift." He uncapped the bottle and lifted it halfway to his mouth. "It's your last one."

King shrugged. "Go ahead." Russ drank. Ginnie was the woman with whom Russ had been having an off-and-on affair—they preferred the word relationship—for the past three or four years. King knew Russ liked it that way, sex and companionship when he wanted it without having to share his home or his life to get it. Ginnie, a natural-born follower, generally did things Russ's way. She wasn't a stupid woman; there had to be some other reason.

Russ embarked on a long, detailed account of exactly how the accident had taken place; but, as usual, the story was more about himself than Ginnie. What he thought, what he said, what he did. He even put down the bottle of beer so his hands would be free to gesture. King didn't know anybody who needed an audience as much as Russ Panuccio did.

"Anyway, I told her I'd take her home tomorrow," Russ finished up. "But I can't stay with her then. There's some stupid-ass function at Pitt I've got to go to. I don't know who thinks these things up. But I have a theory that the administration is secretly convinced the faculty doesn't have enough to do, so they sit around and amuse themselves by inventing useless functions that they then declare mandatory. They—"

"Ginnie's staying in the hospital just the one night?" King interrupted, only half listening.

"I thought they'd put a cast on her leg and let her go, but they don't do it that way anymore. She had to stay overnight so they could check for fever or whatever. I'd forgotten how noisy hospitals can be. I'd hate to spend the night there." Russ tossed the empty bottle into the trash can. "I want another drink. How about coming out to Benny's with me? You don't have anything planned, do you?"

"Well, I've got a stack of journals I—"

"Read them tomorrow. Come on, King, I need company tonight. I also need your bathroom." He strode out of the kitchen.

King sighed. Benny's Bar was a meet-market; it was possible that some people really did go there on Saturday nights just to drink, but somehow King didn't think that was what Russ had in mind. So much for fidelity to poor broken Ginnie. King didn't like Benny's, but he knew he'd end up going.

The truth was, King was worried about turning into a stereotype, the man so in love with his machines that he shut himself away from all human contact. The mad-genius inventor, absorbed in his work, celibate, friendless, a bit of a geek. The cliché image of a near-sociopath, manufactured in Hollywood and never seriously questioned by the easy-answer crowd—which was to say, most of homo sap. Living for one's work struck King as a pretty good way to live, after all. But he couldn't stand the idea of being glibly categorized as an eccentric workaholic. He objected to being categorized at all; categorization was dismissal. As a result he was willing to play straight man to Russ Panuccio on occasion; Russ was not only his closest friend, he was his only friend.

And what did Russ get out of it? Russ got his audience. At one time or another Russ Panuccio had worked as an on-the-air news reporter for every television station in town; but wherever he'd worked, things had a way of not panning out. He'd tried leaving Pittsburgh, anchoring the newscast at some station in Arizona or New Mexico; that didn't last long. Then he was back in Pittsburgh, announcing to the world that his true calling was education. Russ had gone back to school long enough to get an advanced degree and was now teaching journalism at Pitt, a university notoriously indifferent to that subject as a field of proper academic endeavor. But there was just enough interest to keep the ex-newscaster on the payroll, and the captive audiences he met several times a week went a long way toward alleviating Russ Panuccio's obsessive need to be listened to.

But the kids sitting in the classrooms didn't have much choice, and Russ must have been aware of that whether he admitted it or not. So the compulsive talking never did stop, and Russ was always on the lookout for someone's ear to bend; he didn't have many more friends than King did. The two men didn't see each other all that often; but when they did, Russ talked and King listened, or pretended to.

Russ came back into the kitchen talking, complaining about some dean who, according to Russ, had the attention span of a three-year-old. Somehow it was settled without further discussion that King was going to Benny's with him. They got into Russ's car, a Japanese toy that forced King to fold up like an accordion in the passenger seat, and Russ talked them to Benny's Bar in no time flat.

The place was crowded, even though it was still relatively early in the evening. King felt himself cringing at the sight of all those beautified people who'd come to Benny's to see and be seen. At the same time he was fascinated by all the expensive dental work on display; he'd never seen so many sparkling smiles in the same room before in his life. Still, he was planning to slip away after a couple of drinks, if Russ could find what he was looking for fairly fast. A quick survey indicated the women outnumbered the men by a comfortable margin.

"Look for secretaries," Russ instructed. "They're the friendliest."

Curious in spite of himself, King asked, "How do you know which ones are secretaries?"

"They're always the best dressed." The two men made their way to the bar and got their drinks. After his first swallow, Russ cast a practiced eye over the rest of the clientele. "Look over there—two redheads at the same table. And they're alone. Couldn't be better! Come on."

King followed and listened as Russ smoothly complained about the lack of space in Benny's and asked if they would share their table. The women accepted the ploy and the two men sat down.

One of the women watched King fold his long frame into the chair and said, "You have to be a basketball player."

"No."

Awkward pause. Russ shifted his weight and said, "I'm Russ," smiling at both young women.

"And I'm Tiffany."

"I'm Jill."

"King." Even he knew the no-last-name rule.

Tiffany was a secretary, all right, at a big downtown insurance agency. Jill was a doctor's receptionist; close enough. Tiffany was the one who'd asked him if he was a basketball player, but King seemed to be paired off with Jill. She was a pretty girl, a good twenty years younger than he, with carefully mussed salon-red hair and a make-up job that would have had Estée Lauder crowing in triumph. It was only after they'd talked a bit that King realized Jill was shy. But she put a good face on it (literally) and kept up the appearance of a woman of the eighties out having a good time.

He said he was in robotics. She said she'd always been interested in robots. He lied and said he was a Pirates fan. She said she was interested in sports. He said he liked this time of year the best of all. She said she was interested in weather.

That one made him pause. "Do you like your job?" he asked, a bit desperately.

"Oh, yes," Jill beamed, projecting a positive image. "It's very interesting."

". . . and so when you come down to it, it wasn't a difficult decision at all," Russ was saying to a glazed-eyed Tiffany. "I began to get tired of being recognized everywhere I went. When you're on television, your viewers begin to think they own you, you know? Besides, the glitz and the glamor and the big paycheck can get in the way of the truly important things in life. There comes a time when you have to do something for your *soul*—you understand?"

King was embarrassed.

"Interacting with young people—that's much more satisfying than reading news to an audience you can't see." Russ was talking louder now, making sure he could be heard over the rising noise level in the bar. "There's something exciting about watching a young mind awake. Just getting through to the adolescent mind is a challenge . . . I can't live without challenges, can you? God, is it noisy in here! I can barely hear myself think. What say we go someplace quieter where we can talk? I know a nice little spot on the South Side I think you'd like."

The two redheads consulted. "We'll follow you in our car," Tiffany said. Both were smiling bravely.

On the way out, King stopped Jill. "We don't have to go on to another bar if you don't want," he said. "We could, well, we could go to a movie."

"A movie?" Jill echoed dubiously.

"Or dinner. Have you had dinner?"

"Oh, yes. I've had dinner."

"I just meant we didn't have to go bar-hopping if there was something else you'd rather do. We don't have to stick with Russ and, uh, Tiffany."

Her smile had a little hesitation in it. "Well, we both came in Tiffany's car, and . . ."

And you don't know me well enough to go off with me alone. "In that case, we'd all better stay together," he smiled, hoping she noticed how understanding he was being.

The South Side bar, unfortunately, turned out to be even more crowded and noisier than Benny's; so they abandoned it and ended up at the Atrium Lounge of the Sheraton, looking out over the Monongahela River. It was just quiet enough for Russ to continue his monologue.

King labored mightily to carry on a conversation with the shy young receptionist who agreed with everything he said, but it was hard to escape the sound of Russ's voice. Tiffany was struggling to maintain an interested expression. King made what was meant to be a silencing gesture toward Russ but only succeeded in knocking over his drink. A waiter appeared out of nowhere, cleaned up the mess, and silently disappeared. King excused himself and went to the men's room. He needed a breather.

When he came out, he was surprised to see a familiar figure seated at a small table—alone. "Gale? Are you here by yourself? Where's Bill?"

The woman turned and faced him. It wasn't Gale Fredricks.

King stuttered out an apology, feeling a fool. "It's just that you look so much like my assistant," he explained.

"Oh?" the woman said, deadpan. "What does she assist you *with*?"

He relaxed a little. "I design robots."

She smiled wryly. "Well, we can't talk about *that*. I'm a technoklutz myself."

King put on a mournful face. "You don't know how it grieves me to hear that."

"How do you talk to us no-tech types—sign language?"

He pressed his palms together in an attitude of prayerful supplication. The woman who was not Gale laughed and gestured toward the empty chair next to her. King sat down, starting to enjoy himself for the first time that evening.

After fifteen minutes things were going so well that King was emboldened to invite her to his place. He couldn't believe his good luck when she said yes. He paid her bill while she fished car keys out of her purse, and they stood up to leave.

"Going somewhere, Sauerkraut?"

He turned to see Russ glaring at him; King had managed to forget about him without even trying. And the girls—he'd forgotten them as well. "Oh lord, Russ, I'm sorry!" he groaned. "I just now met, er, ah, um."

"You really were going to do it, weren't you?" Russ's voice rose, angry. "You were going to walk out of here without a word—and leave me with both of them! You sonuvabitch. You don't mind shafting me, okay, think of Jill. What you're doing to her is pretty shitty, even for you."

"Look, Russ, I said I was sorry."

"Sorry!" It came out a shout. "Sorry doesn't solve anything!"

"Hey, keep it down, fellas, willya?" a waiter asked with a smile.

Not-Gale stood off to the side listening, a look of amusement on her face.

Russ lowered his voice. "Okay, so you found something better. But what about me? What am I supposed to tell those two back there? My god, King, don't you ever think of anyone but yourself?"

King took a deep breath. "Russ, listen . . . I'm going now. I'm sorry if I've screwed up your plans, but that's the way it is."

He took Not-Gale by the arm and walked out, leaving Russ to handle the Jill problem any way he could.

* 3 *

King Sarcowicz slept until shortly before noon Sunday, waking to feel as if he'd been doped. He squirted toothpaste directly into his mouth and chewed on it morosely before beginning to brush. He had to stoop a little to see all of his face in the bathroom mirror; he'd been meaning to raise the mirror for years but had never got around to it. A hot-and-cold shower got rid of most of the grogginess, and black coffee finished the job. He was depressed. He'd just as soon forget last night, even though it was the first time he'd made love in over a year.

He'd thought it had gone all right; they'd even managed to avoid mentioning the unmentionable—the woman who was not Gale (her name was Teresa) had simply handed him a condom. But then immediately afterward she'd gotten up and dressed. When he asked for her phone number, Teresa had merely smiled enigmatically . . . and left without a word.

So he'd bombed. After Teresa left, it had taken him an hour to get to the point where he was ready to drift off to sleep; but then a racket outside had forced him awake again. He looked through the window to see an ambulance pulled up in Mrs. Rowe's driveway. He dressed hurriedly and went to find out what was the matter. The old lady had had a stroke.

Mrs. Rowe had a Lifecall Medical Relief unit; she'd managed to press the button and help had arrived soon after. King rode in the ambulance with her to Shadyside Hospital, holding the frightened woman's hand and somehow finding the right words to soothe her. At the hospital an Indian doctor told him it could have been worse; Mrs. Rowe would be only partially impaired. The doctor said the old lady was most anxious that someone let her son in Philadelphia know, and also to ask him to come take care of her cat. King said he'd do it, trying not to feel hurt that she'd not trusted him to feed the damned animal. He took the number the doctor gave him and made the call.

Then he'd thought as long as he was in the hospital, he might as well drop in to see Ginnie, Russ Panuccio's now-and-then girlfriend with the broken leg. A nurse had dryly informed him that four A.M. was not included in their regular visiting hours.

King walked home from the hospital, thinking not of Ginnie or Mrs. Rowe or even Teresa but of Russ. Every time King spent an evening with the newscaster-turned-teacher, he was left with a firm resolve to avoid Russ Panuccio assiduously for the next six months. But now he was beginning to regret leaving his "friend" in the lurch earlier that night. If Russ should turn his back on him . . . King wondered what he'd told Jill.

Jill. The toe of his shoe sent a small rock skittering along ahead of him. He took a running start and kicked it lightly, managing to aim it straight down the sidewalk. He was able to keep the rock going for a full block before he lost it in the dark. Jill, Jill. He didn't know her last name and he'd probably never see her again, unless he went looking for her at Benny's and similar Hi-I'm-so-and-so places around town. He wondered if he should. She probably wouldn't even speak to him; her determination to be agreeable couldn't possibly stretch that far. It didn't occur to King to wonder whether he'd be so concerned about Jill if Teresa had given him her phone number. But still he felt ashamed of himself, a little. Dennis Cox had once accused him of being careless with people; King admitted his abandoning of Jill just might possibly fit into that category. *Not a very kingly thing to do.*

By the time he reached home, King's mind had slid away from these minor but seemingly insoluble problems, to dwell instead on major ones for which solutions could reasonably be presumed to exist. He fell asleep thinking about his design for a driverless vehicle and awoke six and a half hours later feeling as if he'd been doped. When his head was clear he went out to buy a Sunday paper—and found himself a sideline observer at the Pittsburgh Marathon.

King was vaguely aware that this thing happened every May, but still it took him by surprise. The enthusiasm of the crowd was contagious, so King lingered a while, standing behind the other spectators and peering over their heads. The runners flew down Walnut Street in Shadyside, all sizes and shapes and ages, both sexes. King was fascinated by one runner who didn't pass by any too quickly; an older man, bald, shirtless, with a salt-and-pepper beard down to his navel. He was laboring. His face and neck were reddish purple, he was covered with sweat, and he was barely jogging, his feet obviously heavy and his strength gone—a coronary in the making if King ever saw one. The guy was killing himself, but he would not quit. *And that kind of determination is undoubtedly admired*, King thought wonderingly. *Insane.* A teen-aged girl in the briefest of shorts passed the bearded man easily.

King stayed until he started to grow thirsty; but back at home he found he was out of beer. He remembered; Russ Panuccio had taken the last one. Into the car, on to Squirrel Hill and Rhoda's Deli. He picked up a loaf of bread but decided against a jar of sour pickles. Beer.

"Heineken, right?" the girl behind the counter said.

"Right."

"Thought so."

King noticed a little smile playing around her mouth. *Pleased with herself—probably wants to be complimented.* He cleared his throat. "Now how did you happen to remember that?"

The smile emerged full-blown. "Oh, I notice faces and I pay attention to what people like and, you know, I remember."

Now what am I supposed to say—congratulations? "Well, ah." He forced a smile.

The girl gave him his change and told him in the sweetest voice imaginable to have a *good* one.

So that's the way the game was played. King grumbled to himself all the way home, knowing that most people would look upon the little scene he'd just acted out as a simple exercise in common courtesy. But he resented having to pretend to be impressed by a countergirl's memory just to win her good will.

With an effort he put aside all thoughts of countergirls and suicidal marathon runners and old women in hospitals and young women with no last names. He spent the rest of the day reading technical journals, and eventually his bad mood passed. It never failed; he was always able to find comfort in a world in which the shortest distance between two points was still one straight unambiguous line.

Gale Fredericks was waiting for him in the laboratory when he got in Monday morning. "I've just been talking to Dennis Cox," she said without preamble. "He tells me we're getting a DARPA contract."

"A piece of one," King smiled, glad to see her after the downer weekend. "A juicy piece, I think."

Her voice had an accusatory tone. "Keystone has never done military work before."

He looked at her curiously. "Of course we have, Gale. Lots of times."

"Not since I've been working here."

King thought back. "That could be," he admitted; the past couple of years all their work had been industrial. "Why, Gale? Is this a problem?"

She slumped down into a chair. "One reason I came to work here was that you told me Keystone didn't do any military work."

Oh-oh. "I may have told you we weren't doing any at the time—I don't remember. You don't want to work on military designs?"

"More than that, I refuse to. And you . . . you shouldn't either. King, you're the closest thing to a genius I've ever met. You don't have to settle for thinking up better ways to kill people. You don't have to do military work."

"But that won't change anything," he objected. "If I don't do it—"

"Somebody else will," she finished for him. "I know, I've heard that song. But *you* don't have to do it."

King couldn't believe this was happening. "Gale, we don't even know what the project *is* yet. It may not be weaponry at all . . . it could be some sort of intelligence-gathering device they want us to design." A picture of his driverless vehicle flashed in his mind. "Or a remote-controlled ambulance—you wouldn't object to working on an ambulance, would you?"

She thought a moment, and then said, "No, I wouldn't object to that."

"Good! Let's wait until Dennis and I meet with MechoTech before we worry about whether we'll be helping kill people or not." He'd meant to make it sound like a joke, but it didn't come out that way. "Gale, don't make any decisions while we're gone. Please?"

She smiled at him. "All right. I'm sorry to dump this on you right before you leave, but I thought you ought to know before you started making plans that'd include me."

"Appreciate it."

Other technicians had begun drifting in with their usual Monday-morning slowness. King and Gale spent some time planning which projects she should ride herd on while he and Dennis were in New York. Then Gale got to work on tracking down the programming error they'd found late Friday afternoon.

King waited until she was deep in her work and said, "I'll be in Dennis's office." She nodded without looking away from her screen.

Dennis's eyes were puffy, as they were every Monday morning. He kept one of them closed as he watched King fold up like a telescope on the chair farthest from Dennis's desk. "Well?" he asked his partner. "Did you think it over?"

King nodded. "Can't do it, Dennis. *I* have to be the one to direct the work."

Dennis grunted, as if expecting that answer. "All right, how about this? You direct the project, but you leave all the workaday decisions to me. Timetables, expenditures, reports to MechoTech and DARPA, whip-cracking, everything. Just the way we do it here. At least we'll present a united front that way."

King let out a sigh of relief; that was exactly what he'd been hoping Dennis would suggest. "Absolutely. No problem."

"That means at times you'll have to take orders from me."

"I can live with it. Just as long as I decide what design work is to be done."

"Agreed." They didn't shake hands on it, mostly because they were on opposite sides of the room. But Dennis was so pleased with having the matter settled that he managed to get his other eye open. "Mimi Hargrove and Gregory Dillard won't have a chance," he grinned. "When it's them against us,

Osterman is gonna pick us."

"We do have a problem, though," King said. "Gale Fredericks. She refuses to have anything to do with military hardware. She may quit."

Dennis swore. "Oh, that's just great, that is. Christ, I didn't know she was a peacenik. Come to think of it, though, she looked at me kind of funny when I told her about the MechoTech project."

"It never came up before because we haven't had a DARPA contract since she started working here."

"Hm. What did you tell her?"

"I put her off. I said wait until we find out what the project is—it might be an automated ambulance or the like."

"Fat chance."

"I know."

Both men were silent. King took out a hardboiled egg and started peeling it; he hadn't taken time for breakfast. Dennis said, "Better start looking for a replacement."

"*After* we've done everything we can think of to keep her," King insisted. "Give her a monster bonus, double her salary, make her a partner—anything."

"Ho, now, wait a minute. Make her a partner?"

"If that's what it takes." King got up and emptied a handful of eggshell fragments in the general direction of Dennis's wastebasket. "She's indispensable, Dennis. And don't argue about it—she *is*. You're the money man. Figure out a way to keep her."

"You're sure money will do it?"

King grimaced. "No. But I don't know what else to offer."

Dennis chewed his bottom lip. "Okay, let me think about it. I'll see what I can come up with."

King muttered his thanks and went out, leaving Dennis glaring at five or six bits of eggshell on his expensive carpet. King ate his egg and tried to think: what other than money might tempt Gale to stay? It came to him as a mild shock that he didn't really know anything about Gale Fredericks except for her work . . . and the fact that she had a husband named Bill. He didn't even know what Bill did for a living. Maybe something there, some help they could give him? If he was in business for himself, for instance, he probably could use some of Keystone's investment capital.

Back in the lab, he waited until his assistant had reached a stopping point before saying, "Gale, I just realized I never asked you—what kind of work does Bill do?"

"He sells computers," she answered absently. "IBM clones mostly. He opened his own business last year."

If she'd glanced up just then, Gale would have been surprised at the size of the smile on her boss's face.

Late Tuesday night, nine hours before he and Dennis were scheduled to take off from Greater Pittsburgh Airport, King suddenly thought about hotel reservations. Panicky, he called his partner to see if he had taken care of them.

"I was wondering if you were going to think of that," Dennis answered with amusement. "Never fear, partner. We are MechoTech's guests. They keep an executive condo just for visiting VIPs like us, ahem. Red carpet treatment."

"Ha!" King exclaimed. "Terrific. I don't like hotels anyway. Where will Mimi and Gregory be staying?"

"Same place." There was a long and ominous silence.

"King?"

"I heard you. Why didn't you tell me before?"

"Because I didn't want to listen to you bitching about it for four days, that's why."

"Shit."

"It might turn out to be a good thing. Maybe you and Mimi can kiss and make up."

"And maybe pigs have wings."

"Come on, King—you're going to be sweet as pie to that woman, aren't you? *Aren't you?*"

"*Yes!*" King yelled, and slammed down the receiver.

The phone rang immediately.

King snatched up the receiver and snarled, "Dennis, I *said* I'd be nice to her!"

"This isn't Dennis, and which 'her' are you referring to?" The broadcaster voice rolled the words out with more resonance than they deserved.

"Oh, Russ, hello. Thought you were my partner."

"I've been waiting to hear from you," Russ said, "but then I realized it would never occur to you to call and apologize."

"I was afraid you'd hang up." It *hadn't* occurred to him. "I am sorry, Russ—I shouldn't have done what I did. Would it help if I gave you my word that it won't happen again?"

"Not much. The damage is done. You made Jill cry, you know."

Somehow King couldn't believe that young Jill had burst into tears at the news of his departure; Russ wasn't above laying a little extra guilt on him for good measure. "What did you tell her?"

"That you'd taken ill and I'd called a cab and sent you home."

"And she didn't believe it?"

"Of course not. She saw you leave with that other woman, uh, what's her name?"

"Teresa. What happened after I left?"

"Why, what do you think happened? I walked the two girls to their car and politely said good night. Tiffany was pissed and Jill was trying not to cry and since you weren't there they took it out on *me*. I want to thank you for one hell of an evening, King."

The sarcasm was deserved, King admitted. "If I could undo it, I would. Did you get their last names? Maybe I could—"

"You think they'd tell me their names after the way you fucked things up? What about this Teresa? Did she give you her last name?"

"Yes," King lied. "It's, ah, Brown."

"Teresa Brown. And her number?"

"Yes, she gave me that too."

"Well, how about sharing? You owe me, after Saturday."

Oh ho, *that* was why he'd called. "I can't do that, Russ."

"Why not? You engaged or something?" Russ's voice turned ugly. "You want to square things, King? This is the way to do it. Give me her number."

King's skin was itching. Trapped in his own lie, he admitted he knew neither Teresa's last name nor where she could be reached—and endured the other man's crowing as stoically as he could. He was slightly affronted by the ease with which Russ accepted this new version of his Saturday night fling.

"So you deserted us for nothing," Russ laughed. "You might as well have stayed."

It wasn't *exactly* for nothing, but something warned him that Russ didn't want to hear that. "Yeah, I might as well have stayed."

Once Russ was convinced that King had struck out too, he was content. He cheerily wished King a good trip before hanging up; they were buddies again.

King went to bed and wasted a good hour's sleeping time cussing into his pillow.

The next morning he left in what he thought was plenty of time, but the airport traffic was so heavy it looked as if everyone in Pittsburgh was catching an early flight that day. He had to wait in line to get into the parking lot, and he just missed the shuttle to the terminal. Rather than wait for the next one he lugged his suitcase to an outside check-in counter. He was sweating by the time he reached the gate, where Dennis was waiting impatiently. All the other passengers had boarded.

"What the hell happened?" Dennis snapped, starting down the boarding tunnel.

"Nothing happened. It just took me this long to get here."

Dennis stepped on the plane. "Thank you," he said to one of the flight attendants.

"Our pleasure," she smiled.

"I had to ask them to hold the plane," Dennis growled to King. "You should have left earlier."

"They'll do that?" King asked, buckling himself in. "Hold a plane if you just ask them to?"

"It's still here, isn't it?" Dennis settled his briefcase on the floor between his feet.

It was still there twenty minutes later. Only when they were airborne did King remember he'd meant to go check on old Mrs. Rowe in the hospital before he left.

"Oh Christ," Dennis moaned as the limo MechoTech had sent to meet them pulled up to the curb. "This isn't their good place—it must be a second one I didn't know about."

It was an older apartment building that had been converted into a condominium, and it looked fine to King. But Dennis, obviously, had been expecting something grander.

"And on the fifth floor, too," he complained on the elevator going up. "We'll get all the street noise."

Mimi Hargrove and Gregory Dillard were already there, having arrived from California the night before. When King and Dennis walked in, the other two were in the living room where the television was tuned to The Movie Channel with the sound turned off. Gregory rose slowly, almost regally. He was a small-boned man, and not very tall; he compensated by making himself exquisitely graceful. He didn't have King's height or Dennis's good looks, but he did have presence. And he loved making bigger men feel clumsy.

There was a moment of awkwardness, with nobody smiling except Dennis. Gregory looked at King with unrevealing eyes; but Mimi didn't look at him at all, even when she spoke. But speak she did, and the initial hurdle was over. Gregory quickly established himself as the one in charge, the host welcoming the newcomers.

How are you, how was your trip. Mimi looked different, King thought, but he couldn't put his finger on what it was. She was as prosperous-looking as ever, as blond as ever, and as California as ever. "You look nice," King told her, unable to think of a more original olive branch.

"Thank you," she said coolly. "You look the same."

He tried again. "Do you have any clue to what MechoTech's giving us, specifically?"

She unbent enough to answer, "Warren Osterman talked to us about so many different possibilities—everything from fiber-optic-guided robots to electromagnetic weapons systems. It's hard to guess which one he finally decided on. What did he say to you?"

"About the same. We're both guessing too."

Dennis, in the meantime, was getting on with Gregory like a house afire. They were laughing and chatting like old friends; it occurred to King that Gregory might be trying to solicit Dennis's support in the coming showdown over who was to head the project. And Dennis . . . what was Dennis doing? King asked Mimi some innocuous question about programming and barely listened to her answer. Mimi or Gregory, Gregory or Mimi— Dennis was right; they'd decided between them which one was better suited for the job than King. All this jockeying for position, even before they knew what they'd be working on.

King couldn't put it off any longer; he had to speak to Gregory. He took a deep breath and went over to stand directly in front of the smaller man. He held out his hand and said,

"Gregory—shake hands. I'm glad to be working with you at last, and I'm hoping you'll let bygones be bygones." Dennis looked surprised.

Smiling as if he knew a secret, Gregory Dillard shook his hand. "That's fine with me, Sauerkraut. Just don't sell me out this time."

"Never. San Francisco was a mistake. I wish to god I'd kept my big mouth shut."

"San Francisco?" Dennis said.

"That could have been a big contract, you know," Gregory went on in a tone of suprisingly mild reprimand.

"I know," King said contritely. "I've been kicking myself ever since."

"Ever since *what?*" Dennis demanded.

Mimi was the only one to pay any attention to him. "Your partner diverted some business away from us—just by saying the wrong thing at the right time, evidently. I wasn't there. It was Gregory he pulled the rug from under."

Dennis looked daggers at King. "And everybody knew about it except me? Wonderful."

King was still trying to convince Gregory of his sincerity. "There was nothing malicious about it, Gregory. I just didn't think. I'll do anything to make up for it."

Gregory looked at him slyly. "Anything? Then turn down the directorship of the project."

Pow. King smiled uneasily, thinking he'd walked right into that one. "You don't beat around the bush, do you? All right, now it's out in the open. Every one of us wants to head this project, right? Well, I propose that we agree right now to accept Warren Osterman's decision unanimously. If he picks one of you, I'll go along with it. By the same token, if I get the nod— you don't challenge his choice. Agreed?"

Mimi laughed shortly. "That's hardly a generous offer, King. These projects almost invariably go to the head designer."

"Yes, but you've been working on Osterman, haven't you?" he asked with a flash of insight. "And I haven't. That should even our chances pretty well, I'd think."

The two from SmartSoft admitted nothing, neither by word nor expression. King smiled at them pleasantly, but inwardly he was in turmoil. The president of MechoTech *had* to see that only the head designer could direct the sort of complex work they'd be doing; if his evaluation of Warren Osterman's perceptiveness was wrong, King might have just handed the project over to Mimi and Gregory.

Help came from Dennis Cox. "Hey, folks, I don't count myself out of the running—but it seems to me King's suggestion is the only sensible course to follow. Whoever heads up the project, we're going to have to find a way to work together. Christ, it's not going to be all that hard. Tell you what. Give King and me some time to get settled in, and then we'll do lunch. We don't have to be at MechoTech until three."

"Lunch sounds good," Mimi said quickly, either because she was hungry or because she was playing for time.

Thinking that he really ought to learn how to 'do' a lunch sometime, King looked at his watch. "Isn't it kind of early to eat?"

Shut up, King, Dennis's look said. "How about it, Gregory?"

Gregory smiled only with his mouth. "Lunch, by all means. And of course we'll find a way to work together, that goes without saying. But I can't help but wonder whether King has taken into consideration all the responsibilities that go with running a project as big as this one evidently is—not only the kinds of responsibilities but the sheer number of them as well."

"Tell him at lunch," Dennis urged. "Right now, we'd better unpack. How many bedrooms does this place have?"

The apartment had six bedrooms, but one of them had been turned into an office; it held a conference table, a supply cabinet, and three computer terminals. Of the remaining five bedrooms, only two had attached baths; Mimi and

Gregory had taken those.

"So we have to go down to the end of the hall to pee," Dennis said, still grousing about not being quartered in MechoTech's impress-the-hell-out-of-'em condo. "We might as well be in a boarding house."

"The bathroom—which end of the hall?" King asked.

"Ah, there seems to be one at each end. At least we don't have to share. But we don't even have computers in our rooms! Just those three in the office. And look at this." He went into the bedroom he'd chosen and picked up a bright red Japanese-made mini-television, complete with antenna and four-inch screen. "They really outdid themselves, didn't they? Not even cable TV. Shit."

"There's cable in the living room."

"Oh wow, aren't we the lucky ones. I'll bet you anything you like that the guys from the Defense Department weren't put up here."

King shrugged and went into his own bedroom to unpack. It was a comfortable room; it had everything he needed. The only difference from Dennis's room was that his mini-TV was black instead of red.

When they both were squared away, they went back into the living room to find Mimi and Gregory at a window, both of them looking straight down.

"What's going on?" Dennis asked.

"Come take a look," Gregory said. "Easy—don't scare her."

On the ledge outside was a dull-coated pigeon; a more brightly colored male fluttered anxiously nearby.

"It's a pigeon," Dennis said, his voice implying *So?*

"She has only one foot," Mimi said.

It was true; the bird still had both legs, but the claw was missing from the end of one of them. As they watched, the pigeon waddled along the edge, her body tipping precariously to the side when she put her weight on her stump. King felt strange watching her.

"Maybe she's hungry," Gregory said to Mimi. "Did we eat all the bagels?"

"I think there's one left."

Gregory went to the kitchen to see. Dennis, uninterested in handicapped birdlife, flopped down on the sofa and stared at the silent TV screen, now showing a fantasy film. Gregory came back with the bagel.

The window was one of the old-fashioned kind that opened from the bottom. King turned the lock at the top; but when he tried to lift the window, he couldn't. "It's stuck."

"These older buildings all have windows that are hard to open," Mimi said with a sigh. "Here, let's both try."

They each took a handle and heaved; together they got the window open . . . with a loud *screeeech* that startled everybody. Alarmed, the lame pigeon took flight, followed closely by her mate.

"At least nothing's wrong with her wings," King said as he watched the two birds soar out of sight.

"Ah, that's too bad," Gregory said regretfully. "I'll put some crumbs out anyway—maybe they'll come back. Hold the window."

Easier said than done. The window was heavy, incredibly heavy; King and Mimi were both straining as Gregory leaned out over the windowsill to scatter bagel crumbs along the ledge. He pulled back in; the other two started to lower the window . . . but it got away from them and fell into place with a crash.

"Christ!" Dennis yelped.

"I'm surprised the glass didn't break," Gregory murmured, unruffled. "Everybody all right?"

Everybody was all right, and everybody was suddenly famished. Mimi got her purse but then paused. "Do you mind waiting while I make a phone call? I want to leave a message for Michael." Her husband.

Of course no one minded. But Mimi's mention of her husband reminded King of one very important social amenity he'd neglected: always ask about their spouses. He faced Gregory and said, "How's Sharon?"

"Karen. She's fine."

Whoops. King grinned inanely, unable to think of anything more to say.

Gregory gave him a superior smile that made King feel like a graceless dolt. Then the smaller man turned his back to King and started talking to Dennis. He was talking *at* him, King quickly realized, smoothly and energetically, without giving Dennis time to answer. It wasn't often he saw Dennis Cox playing straight man; but now his partner was reduced to saying *Oh?* and *Yes* and *Well, I* . . . as Gregory delivered what amounted to a monologue. There was a lot of Russ Panuccio in Gregory Dillard.

Mimi finished her phone call and they left the building. Once they were out in the pleasant May sunshine, Gregory decided there was no hurry. They took their time, stopping to look at anything that caught Gregory's eye. Gregory decided which direction they'd walk in, when they'd cross a street or turn a corner. Nobody seemed to mind except Dennis. "Kind of full of himself, isn't he?" he muttered to King.

Eventually they came to restaurant that looked inviting; they were early enough that the place wasn't crowded yet. The beige tablecloths and generally muted décor were exactly what Gregory was looking for, he said. They slid into a semicircular booth. Still asserting his leadership, Gregory ordered martinis for all of them. Dennis quickly countermanded the order and asked for a whiskey sour. King pressed his lips together to keep from laughing; Dennis never drank anything but martinis at lunch.

"Mimi, you look different," King said amiably, "but I can't figure out how."

"I'm the same as always," she said. "You know, that one-footed pigeon upset me."

A waiter put an industrial-strength martini in front of King and a different waiter handed him a roadmap-sized menu. King glanced hopelessly through the list of entrées and asked for a mushroom omelet.

"Christ, King, haven't you ever heard of green vegetables?" Dennis snapped. "Or meat?"

Mimi sighed. "I do wish you'd stop saying *Christ* all the time."

"Huh. God Junior. Is that better?"

Gregory pretended to find that amusing. Mimi did not. Thoroughly out of temper by now, Dennis buried himself in the menu and ordered lamp chops and asparagus. Gregory ordered lamb chops and salad. Mimi ordered salad.

King conjectured that Dennis was sniping at him because he didn't have the nerve to take on Gregory Dillard. His spirits sank; he was afraid that today was just a foretaste of the way it was going to go with the four of them. King didn't have the tact to handle such tender egos; he foresaw a long period of squabbling and backbiting and wondered if Keystone and SmartSoft could ever merge into an effective team. Whichever project Warren Osterman was going to offer them, it had better be worth it.

Whatever it was.

* 4 *

Only a few of the nation's robot manufacturers had established corporate headquarters in New York City; by and large they found it more practical to maintain offices at the sites of the manufacturing plants themselves. MechoTech Corporation had fifty-five such plants, the nearest in Parsippany, New Jersey; but its corporate headquarters sat high up in the Bellows-Wright Building in midtown Manhattan. King Sarcowicz stood at a floor-to-ceiling window in one of MechoTech's conference rooms and experienced a twinge of vertigo.

They were waiting for Warren Osterman to make his appearance; King was glad of a moment or two to orient himself. MechoTech was forever rearranging its office floor plan and nothing was ever where it had been the last time he'd been there. One thing King did like about the place, though, was the fact that there were no cute little robots rolling around bearing trays of drinks or whatever.

"Long way down." Gregory Dillard had joined him at the window. Gregory lowered his voice and asked, "Do you know what's bugging Dennis? He's been glowering at me ever since lunch."

Maybe he doesn't like being one-upped. King looked down at the top of Gregory's head and said, "No idea."

"Did I say something? Did I do something?" Gregory was not in the least concerned about whether he'd offended Dennis or not; he was just well into his I-am-on-top-of-it mode. "If I did, I'd like to set it right."

King simply shrugged, not much inclined to smooth things over for either of them. He turned from the window and glanced at the other two in the room. At that moment Dennis Cox and Mimi Hargrove were doing something that looked suspiciously like flirting. That was surprising, considering how heavily married Mimi was.

The door opened and Warren Osterman walked in. Nearing seventy, Osterman had hair so black it could only have been dyed. He was dressed in a tan pinstripe suit, a brown shirt, and a white tie. He was short, squat, and ugly. He looked like a gangster.

As self-appointed spokesman, Gregory advanced toward Osterman with his hand extended and words of appreciation for This Great Opportunity in his mouth. Osterman shook his hand perfunctorily, spoke to Mimi and Dennis, and turned his attention to King.

"Hello, Warren," King said, pleased at seeing the old gangster again.

"Well, King, are you ready for a challenge?" Osterman smiled. "I've got one for you that's already defeated four design teams."

"Chompin' at the bit."

"Then let's get at it." Osterman turned and pointed at a woman who had followed in his wake and whom none of the others had noticed. "You all know Rae Borchard." King didn't. "She's going to be coordinating your project. You got problems—take 'em to Rae."

Before anyone else could say anything, Gregory slid forward and gracefully took one of her hands in both of his. "Rae, this is a pleasure. I'm looking forward to working with you."

"Thank you," the woman said expressionlessly, and did not return the compliment.

Dennis Cox smothered a laugh. "Let's sit," Warren Osterman commanded, taking his place at the head of the conference table. The woman named Rae Borchard sat to Osterman's right and King sat next to her; she was fortyish, but that was about all her appearance told about her—except that her looks were a bit quiet compared to Mimi's California brightness. Mimi was directly across the table from King, with Gregory on one side of her and Dennis on the other. Before each place was a legal pad and four newly sharpened pencils; King clasped his hands between his knees, not wanting to doodle during a meeting as important as this one.

Face-to-face with Mimi, King at last realized what was different about her: her hair. It was bigger. Mimi's face was rather narrow, and she now wore a compensatory hairdo that drew attention away from that narrowness. Her hair on each side of her head was exactly the same width as her face. King was so bemused by this tripartite structure of west hair, face, east hair, that he missed part of Warren Osterman's opening remarks.

". . . and you're all free to reject the project I'm going to offer you, of course," Osterman was saying. "There'll be no hard feelings. But I don't think you're going to want to pass this one up. The Department of Defense has decided to go for broke. They're proceeding on the assumption that the battlefield of the future will be close to one hundred percent lethal. If a soldier is seen, he will be killed."

Dennis cleared his throat. " 'Seen' by . . . personnel? Or machines?"

"By machines. Mobile intelligence-gathering units, eye-spy orbitals, heat-sensing devices, you name it. Once one of those gizmos fingers one of our soldiers, he's had it. So the obvious solution is to remove the soldier from the direct-fire zone. Put him in a control unit and let him deploy his weapons from a distance. The next big war will be fought by remote control."

"Machines fighting machines," Gregory murmured.

"That's about it. The next war is going to be unbelievably destructive, in terms of both the natural environment and manmade structures. Our job is to keep the army alive and functioning." Osterman went on to explain that MechoTech was contracted to manufacture several different offensive systems the Defense Department had decided were bound to be the most effective, all of them robots of one kind or another. "Defense has abandoned the idea of a central supercomputer controlling an entire battle from one spot. Instead they want a series of interlinked computers that process in parallel. That way if part of the system goes down, other parts can take over its functions."

Mimi asked, "Is all this to be under the control of an artificial intelligence?"

Osterman looked at Rae Borchard, who answered the question. "No, AI will be used in support only—to alert the operator to the most threatening target or solve the allocation-of-fire problem and perform similar functions. It'll need to project probable outcomes of several available firing patterns and then recommend one. I have all the specifications here." She distributed binders holding three inches of paper to each of them. "But all the decision-making will be done by the human operator. AI will function in an advisory capacity only."

Mimi smiled. "Good. Sometimes Defense has an unrealistic picture of what machine intelligence can do."

"Not anymore," Osterman interjected. "They've gotten pretty sophisticated in the ways of robots and their programming. So by now you should be getting an idea of how big this project is. We're subcontracting forty-two different companies just to work on optics alone. I forget the number we've got working on acoustic sensors—Rae?"

"Nineteen," she said without hesitation.

Osterman nodded. "Nineteen. Anyway, I've already got MechoTech's designers at work on refining a robot tank that nobody's been able to perfect in nearly twenty years of trying. And you four," he grinned at them, "you four get the plum. Defense is convinced that a fully automated, remote-controlled weapons platform will be what determines the winner in future ground wars. They're going to build their entire land-based defense system around it."

"A weapons platform," King repeated. "What kind of weapons?"

Rae Borchard answered him. "The people behind the Army Tactical Command and Control Systems in Washington have spent a lot of time trying to find the best weapons for field artillery as well as maneuver control and logistics manipulation. And they've decided the answer is electromagnetic guns."

King shook his head. "Capacitor storage. Takes up too much space."

"Maxwell Lab in San Diego pretty much has that problem licked," Rae said. "The components are getting smaller with each new generation. Right now you could build an electromagnetic gun platform no bigger than an M1 Abrams tank."

King hadn't known that. Excited, he pulled his legal pad toward him and started sketching. A lot of external work had to be taken care of before he could get down to the nuts and bolts of making it work—silhouette, for example. Tall and skinny for maneuvering through wooded areas, as flat as possible for open-field firing. Also, near-instantly changeable means of locomotion to match a changing terrain: desert, marsh, rocky areas, jungle.

Osterman smiled a gangster smile in King's direction and said, "You ought to be able to use the image-enhancement and other visuals already developed by the folks we've got doing optics for the robot tank and a couple of other things. We even stole the guys who were working on the mobile land mines. But Defense doesn't want to depend on optics alone. The optics people have worked wonders in improving resolution even under bad lighting conditions, but they can't do anything about removing obstructions to the line of sight. So we're going to have to come up with reliable tactile sensors."

Ha! King thought. *I knew it!*

"If you need something more specialized than what we've already got in development," Osterman continued, "let Rae know and we'll subcontract the firm that can provide it. The point is, we've got to get this baby right. Because the quality control is going to be *rigid*." Osterman paused for a breath. "Defense has been caught with egg on its face just once too often. They don't want any more turkeys like the Bradley Fighting Vehicle or the Aegis Radar Detection System showing them up. The time when no one gave a damn whether a weapon worked or not just so long as everybody made a little pocket change out of it—well, those gravy days are over. Too many watchdogs now. So . . . no short cuts, people."

Dennis asked, "Who's doing the mobile land mines?"

"Automated America," Osterman answered. A Japanese-owned firm. "Personally, I think that one's going to be a dead end. But as long as it keeps the competition busy and out of our hair, I'm not going to say so where anybody can hear me."

King looked up from his sketching. "Supply? How are these platforms to be kept supplied with ammo?"

"That's part of the project, a supplier and loader. Find a way."

King nodded and turned back to his sketches. He needed another legal pad for notes; without looking up he reached out and took Rae Borchard's. Rae didn't notice; she was busy passing out the folders containing the minimum specifications Defense insisted on.

Osterman spent some time speaking about various technical requirements, his voice rumbling like a worn-out machine. "Rae's also got reports on earlier attempts to meet all these specs. Earlier failures, that is. They might save you some time." She passed them out, and Osterman glanced at King, amused that the latter was already on the job. "Dennis, I hope you're getting all this because I'm not sure your partner is."

"I'm listening," King said without looking up.

Mimi was reading something in the specifications folder. "Warren . . . Defense wants computers in the control units that are voice-responsive?"

"Right. Defense figures there are going to be so many screens to watch at once that the soldier-operator won't have time to type out instructions. They're planning on using Carnegie Mellon's Sphinx—another DARPA project."

Gregory waved a small hand dismissively. "That won't work," he said. "The Sphinx computer is still talking baby talk. I attended a demonstration at CMU, and the poor thing got confused by the different accents people have. It couldn't understand Southern at all."

So Gregory's been in Pittsburgh recently, King thought and then carelessly dropped his pencil. When he bent down to pick it up, he looked under the table and was surprised to see Dennis's hand in Mimi's lap. Her legs were just far enough apart to give him room. King barely avoided bumping his head when he straightened up.

"That must have been an early demonstration you saw," Rae was saying to Gregory. "The computer now recognizes eight basic groups of dialects, and its vocabulary keeps growing each day. Sphinx will be ready before we are."

Gregory smiled at her. "You guarantee that?"

She smiled back. "I guarantee nothing."

"Guarantees or no guarantees," Osterman said, "Sphinx is what Defense wants to use, so you'll have to program for it.

Before we go any further with the specs, though, you'll want some time to study them as well as Rae's reports on our other projects that may have applications you can use. Say we meet again at two tomorrow—that should give you time to familiarize yourself with enough of the details that we can get down to specifics. Agreed?"

They all agreed.

Osterman paused. "There's one more matter before we break up for today. King, put your pencil down. I want your full attention for this."

King obediently put his pencil down.

"I want it understood once and for all," Osterman said, "that King Sarcowicz is project leader here. You other three—every one of you has approached me about replacing him. The answer is still no."

King shot an anguished look at Dennis, who wouldn't meet his eye.

Osterman noticed. "That's right, King—your partner too. They're all worried about your organizational abilities. But you're the talent that's going to solve the robot problems if they can be solved, so you're the one who's going to run this show, not some superefficient pencil-pusher. If you get behind in the paperwork, hire someone to take care of it."

Gregory coughed discreetly. "It's not just that, Warren. When Mimi and I design the circuitry for computer control of the platform, we'll need to have thought out our software program completely so that the two are compatible. How you design the hardware of anything is determined by the instructions you use to operate that hardware. The program design *must* precede everything else." He coughed again. "And that's why this project should be under Mimi's direction instead of King's."

King grinned at Mimi, self-confident in victory. "You won the toss, huh?" She stared at him. He remembered, too late, how utterly humorless a woman she was.

Osterman smiled pleasantly at the two from SmartSoft. "Programming *über alles*, is that it? I know you sold that bill of goods to the Navy once, but it won't work here. You come up with the software to fit King's designs, King's and Dennis's—not the other way around. That's so obvious I'm surprised we're even talking about it."

"It's not a bill of goods, Warren," Gregory replied smoothly, showing no sign of taking offense. "It's a fact of life. If—"

"No, Gregory. *King is in charge.* End of discussion." There was a moment of uncomfortable silence. Osterman didn't have to threaten to replace Gregory and Mimi if they gave him any flak; they all knew he'd do it in a flash if he felt that would help the project. So King had won the battle without having to fire a shot. He noticed the woman next to him watching the interchange closely, her face expressionless. Whoever Rae Borchard was, she wasn't giving much away about herself.

Warren Osterman murmured a few professional words of reconciliation and the meeting was over. King felt like a schoolboy again as he started gathering up notepads, folders, and the heavy binders full of papers. He'd forgotten to bring a briefcase, but he hid a smile when he saw the other three weren't able to fit all these new documents into the cases they did remember to bring. Loaded down, all four of them stood helplessly before the conference room door. Rae opened it and let them out.

"Pit stop," Gregory said.

Mimi nodded. The two of them went off in search of rest rooms, leaving King and Dennis alone. King looked at the other man and said, "*Et tu*, partner?"

Angrily Dennis charged away toward the elevators, King close behind. The elevator buttons were the heat-activated kind, so King leaned over his armful of papers and breathed on the down button. "So what was all that crap you were giving me right before we left, about how you'd take care of the day-to-day stuff running the project and—"

"That's what I'm going to end up doing anyway, isn't it?" Dennis snapped. "You really think I enjoy doing all your grunge work while you go airily on your way, thinking Great Thoughts and getting all the credit?" He snorted. "You wouldn't even be here now if it weren't for me."

The arrival of the elevator cut off King's reply. The car already held four passengers, so King and Dennis rode down in stony silence. King sneaked a peek at his partner; Dennis was not looking his usual handsome self. His face was not contorted, but it was different; King didn't know another person whose physiognomy could be so subtly altered by anger. They both needed time to cool off.

Out on the street, they had trouble getting a cab. They both yelled "Taxi!" at the passing yellow vehicles, which continued to pass. Dennis stepped out into the street and tried jumping up and down; no luck.

King looked over the crowd on the sidewalk and picked out an older woman who was carrying a folded umbrella in each hand, like weapons. He stopped her and said, "Lady, would you get us a cab? Please? Our arms are full."

The woman looked up at King towering over her and juggling his bushel of papers. She nodded and stepped off the curb, raised one of the umbrellas in the air, and popped it open. A cab braked in front of her.

"Thanks," King muttered as he climbed in after Dennis, who gave the driver the address of the MechoTech apartment and then stared silently out the window.

King's skin was getting that crawly, itchy feeling he hated. He swallowed nervously and said, "I think you owe me an explanation."

"What's to explain?" Dennis answered sourly. "I made my pitch and I lost. What have you got to complain about? You're in the catbird seat."

He sounds as if he hates me, King thought wonderingly. "Dennis—what you said back there, by the elevator. I know I wouldn't be here if it weren't for you. I could never have made it on my own. I need someone to, uh—"

"You need someone to baby-sit you, that's what you need," Dennis said unpleasantly. He made his hand into a gun and pointed it at King. "You have a child's understanding of responsibility, King, and I'm getting goddam tired of leading you by the hand."

And then always coming in second-best? "Dennis, I'm sorry you feel that way—"

"I'm sure you are." Bitter.

"We can work it out, you'll see. If we both . . . whoa, wait a minute. What the hell am I apologizing to you for? You're the one who tried to sell *me* out, goddammit!"

"Oh, give it a rest," Dennis said tiredly. "We're not going to settle anything this way."

The cab let them out. They rode up in the elevator without meeting each other's eyes, and once inside Dennis went straight to his room and closed the door. King headed for the room that had been turned into an office and dumped his armload of documents on the conference table. Within five minutes Dennis was forgotten as King buried himself in the details of the problems inherent in making electromagnetic gun platforms work.

The three men had the place to themselves that evening; Mimi was spending the night at the Jade East at JFK Airport. "Her husband's stopping over for just this one night," Gregory explained to King and Dennis. "Michael's on his way to Vienna and then on to the Indian Ocean, to look for some very important fish that everybody thought was extinct." He gave a superior smile. "I presume it will prove we're descended from God instead of from Cheetah." Gregory thought anthropology was a quaint profession.

"What about all the stuff Osterman gave us to read?" Dennis asked.

"She took it with her."

Dennis snickered. "Any bets on how much work she gets done?"

"Oh, I think it's Michael who'll be doing all the work."

King didn't like this *at all*. "Can we forget Mimi's sex life and get back to business?" He waited until he was sure he had their attention and said, "We're responsible for three separate units—the weapons platform, the ammo supplier and loader, and a control unit directing both of them. We can forget about the last two for the time being. Have you had a chance to study the capacitor storage specs?"

They plugged away at the mountain of material Rae Borchard had distributed earlier, assimilating part of it but passing over most of the details. Dennis wanted to study what hadn't worked before, so they wouldn't make the same mistakes. King was more inclined to start from scratch and use the records of past failures as a simple reference, like a roadmap of directions to avoid. Gregory saw everything in terms of programming.

At eleven o'clock Dennis stood up and stretched. "God, my back is hurting!"

"It's been a long day," Gregory agreed. "I don't know about you two, but I've had it for now. I'm going out to get a drink, maybe a bite to eat. Dennis?"

Dennis rubbed the small of his back and said, "Yeah, I'm coming." Neither man asked King to join them.

When they were gone, King decided to put the rough sketches he'd made during the conference at MechoTech into some kind of order. The first of the office's three computers had no CAD program but the second one did. King was mulling over the driverless vehicle he'd been working on at home. How best to use it? He could turn over what he'd done so far to the MechoTech designers working on the robot tank. Or . . . he could try to adapt it to the platform and ammo-loader. Obviously the thing to do was keep it to himself for the time being. The CAD program in the computer was a familiar one, so he was able to get to work immediately. He became so engrossed in what he was doing that he didn't hear Dennis and Gregory when they came back a couple of hours later.

The last one to bed, King was the last to rise the next morning. He dressed and stumbled down the hall to the bathroom. When he came out he bumped into Dennis just leaving his room. Dennis was barefooted and wearing a robe, and he carried the little red four-inch TV from his room.

"We've got a problem at home," King greeted him. "Gale Fredericks. She's not going to be any too happy about the weapons platform."

"Yeah, I've been thinking about that. We'll just have to put some money in her husband's business after all."

"Good. How much should I tell her we're—"

"You tell her nothing. *I* tell the husband we're interested in investing and let *him* work on her. You keep out of it."

King nodded agreement, secretly relieved. "She might come around, you never know. Once she hears we've got the plum assignment—"

Dennis snorted. "Plum assignment my ass! Why do you think Warren gave the EM gun platform to us instead of his own designers? Because MechoTech doesn't want the damned thing. We didn't get the plum—we got the lemon."

King grimaced. "It won't be as hard as all that."

"Four teams, King. Four other teams tried and couldn't get it to work."

King didn't want to argue. He looked at the small red television set his partner was carrying and said, "Where are you taking the TV?"

"To the bathroom—this one." Dennis pointed his gun hand toward the bathroom King had just vacated. "My back's killing me this morning. I'm going to have to soak for at least an hour, so you use the other bathroom, down there."

"Okay. Hope your back gets better."

Dennis made a *hunph* sound and went into the bathroom. King headed toward the kitchen, where he was happy to find a carton of eggs in the refrigerator. He cooked four, sunny-side up, and made some toast. He was just finishing when Gregory came in, looking as excited as Gregory ever looked.

"She's back!" he said to King. "Give me some bread."

"Money bread or bread bread? Who's back?"

"Our one-footed pigeon. She's on the ledge now and I want to feed her."

King handed over a slice of bread and asked, "What's this fascination with pigeons?"

"Oh, I love all birds—I can watch them for hours. They're so graceful, you know. Not at all like people." He flitted out of the kitchen.

King ground his teeth and followed Gregory to the living room. From the bathroom came the sound of gunfire and squealing tires; Dennis was settled in for his hour-long soak.

King and Gregory peered down through the window. Sure enough, the limping pigeon and her mate were both on the ledge that circled the building not far below. Every time she took a step on her stump, King's ankles ached. There was no sign of yesterday's bagel crumbs, which had either been eaten or had blown away.

Gregory put down his slice of bread and grasped one of the window's two handles with his small-boned hands. "Remember the noise it made yesterday. Try to *ease* it up."

King took the other handle, and together the two men slowly lifted the heavy window. It made a slight screech, but not enough to scare off the two birds on the ledge below. When they had it high enough, King shifted his grip so that he was holding the window by its bottom frame.

"Got it?"

"If you hurry," King grunted, straining. "It's damned heavy."

Gregory leaned out over the sill and started tearing his slice of bread into smaller pieces. King gritted his teeth and concentrated on holding the window steady.

The phone rang.

King's head automatically swiveled toward the mechanical sound . . . and in that moment of inattention to what he was doing, he felt the window begin to slip out of his hands. "*Gregory!*" he screamed.

Gregory jerked back in at the sound of King's scream—but he wasn't fast enough. The falling window hit him in the nape of his neck with a sickening sound. Gregory's feet slipped out from under him as the window forced his head down, to come to a stop with a thud and the sound of something breaking. King stared horrified at the half-severed neck, the head dangling outside, the dead eyes open.

The phone was still ringing. From the bathroom came the sound of gunfire and squealing tires.

Paralyzed and helpless, King watched as the window seemed to give a sigh and settled all the way down. Gregory's head dropped to the ledge, frightening away the pigeons, and then rolled over the edge to fall to the street below. King squeezed his eyes shut, but still his mind provided him with a picture of the impact a human head would make on a sidewalk after a fall of five stories.

A wave of nausea swept over him that made his head spin and his legs turn to rubber. Half-blind with shock, King stumbled across the room, crashing into furniture and banging his head against a door when he opened it. Out in the hallway his legs gave way altogether. On his hands and knees he crawled to the bathroom and pushed the door open.

"Oh, for Christ's sake, King!" Dennis snapped. "I told you to use the other one! What are you doing?"

King half rose to lurch toward the toilet. He flung out his arms to keep himself from falling again, knocking something off the toilet tank lid in the process. He bent over the bowl and started throwing up—first that morning's eggs and toast and later just bile. He vomited so hard it was coming out of his nose as well as his mouth. He heaved and heaved until there was nothing left.

He rested his forehead against the seat a moment, and then reached out for some toilet paper to wipe his mouth and nose. The toilet was right next to the bathtub; he flushed and slowly eased himself up to sit on the side of the tub, his back to Dennis. Every part of his body was shaking. But he was going to have to face Dennis; he was going to have to tell him what had happened.

Heavily he turned toward his partner. At first King didn't understand what he saw. Dennis was lying utterly motionless in the tub, both his mouth and his eyes open. Oddly, he didn't seem to be breathing. Between his feet in the water rested the red four-inch television set. *That* was what King had knocked off the toilet tank lid. There was a smell of burning in the air.

Then he understood. Dennis was dead. And King had killed him.

Totally numbed, King sat there a long time, looking at his dead partner. Then he slowly got up and went to the washbasin. He washed his face and hands and used Dennis's toothbrush to clean his teeth. He stared at his image in the mirror and thought: *So that's what shock looks like.*

He left the bathroom and went into Dennis's room. The bed wasn't made. Then he went into the kitchen, where he opened the refrigerator door and closed it again. He wandered into the office, powered up all three computers, and wandered out again.

I've got to tell somebody, King thought. Warren Osterman, the police, somebody. But how could he? How could he admit that *he* . . . before he could complete the thought, the phone rang again. This time the sound scared him. He backed away from the phone; he couldn't talk to anybody, he couldn't *face* anybody.

Not after what he had done.

King Sarcowicz bolted. He staggered out of the apartment and beat his fist against the elevator button. He looked at the lights over the doors and saw the elevator was already on its way up.

People. He couldn't face people yet.

Wildly he looked around for a stairway . . . over there. He pushed through the door and stumbled down the stairs, flight after flight, as fast as his feet could carry him.

He ran.

* 5 *

The fireworks going off in King's head shut out most of the street noise; he ran a block, then jogged a block, and then gradually settled down to a hard-breathing walk. The air was thick with exhaust fumes; a siren was wailing. Strangers jostled him, and an adolescent boy tried to sell him something. In his flight to avoid facing people, King found himself surrounded by them.

He didn't know where he was going. *DennisDennisDennis* his head pounded, and once in a while *Gregory*. He paused a moment to watch an elderly man and woman arguing, on the verge of coming to blows. "I've killed two men," he told them plaintively. Nobody paid any attention.

King let himself be borne along by the forever-changing mob of pedestrians. When they crossed the street, he crossed the street; when they stopped, he stopped. He didn't know whether he was headed uptown or down, and he didn't care. The fireworks inside his head gradually began to die down and the traffic noise took over. In one part of his mind King marveled at the casual way the people on the sidewalk brushed against him; he was contaminated, and he felt surprised they couldn't see it.

All at once he began to feel suffocated. He broke away from the mob and bolted down one of the side streets, which turned out to be no less crowded than the street he'd left. He ran for two long blocks before he started slowing down, weaving his way among the other pedestrians. Up ahead he could see the river. He didn't know which river.

Eventually the street came to an end. King crossed under a rusting elevated highway and found himself facing a series of blue street barriers. Low ones, though, less than three feet high; they didn't even come up to his crotch. He stepped over the barriers and ended up on a pier—Pier 97, a sign said. He couldn't see any ships. Not a single ship, but all the free space on the pier was taken up by parked garbage trucks. Unhappy, King squeezed among the trucks and worked his way toward the end of the pier; he sat down on a bollard, dizzy and exhausted.

Whether this was the East River or the Hudson, it gave off a pronounced stench. A stinking river in front of him and garbage trucks behind him—they suited his mood. He looked across the water at either New Jersey or Queens, he couldn't be sure which. He wasn't far enough downtown for it to be Brooklyn, he was sure; besides, he'd recognize the Brooklyn Bridge if he saw it. It looked like New Jersey. That was important, wasn't it? Figuring out where he was?

No, it was not important. It was a diversionary tactic, a way of keeping from thinking about what he'd done to Dennis Cox and Gregory Dillard. How could one man's casual clumsiness so easily end the lives of two other people? If he hadn't turned his head when the phone rang . . . if he'd paid more attention to where his hands were going when he bent over the toilet bowl to throw up . . . he wanted to throw up again, but there was nothing left in his stomach. He gave in to self-loathing, feeling heavy and bowed down.

King thought of his mother. He could imagine her horror, her *disgust,* if she had lived to see what he'd done this day. No simple headshake of disapproval this time. She'd surely go into shock to think that a son of hers could, simply by not paying attention to what he was doing, cause the deaths of two people. How fragile life was! How easily shattered! How much *care* was needed all the time, not to harm and not to destroy. *You're careless with people,* Dennis had said.

King edged off the bollard and sat on the very end of the pier, his legs dangling in the air. *On his feets uneven.* He stared down into the dirty water and thought how simple it would be just to slip off the pier and put an end to it. How could he live with the shame of what he'd done? King buried his face in his hands, hiding himself from the world. After a period of shuddering, he took his hands down and clasped them tightly between his knees, hunching his long frame over into as small a mass as he could manage. It was an interesting, semifetal position he found himself in; all he had to do was tip forward a little more . . . and into the river he'd go.

He sat like that for a long while, poised between a decisive, irrevocable act and the muddled mess his life had become. He sat there until the sun was almost directly overhead. He was uncomfortably warm. His stomach growled.

At last he leaned back away from the end of the pier, bracing his weight on his arms behind him. It occurred to him that if he just slipped into the water, he might pop up to the surface again like a cork. If he were going to do this, he'd need something to weight himself down. He glanced vaguely around the pier-turned-parking-lot but could see no ropes or heavy rocks handy. Not even a rusty anchor left behind on this shipless pier. But what if he did find something for weight, what then? The ropes would come loose, or the weight wouldn't be heavy enough, or the foul water would make him gag and he'd fight like the devil to get out. One way or another, he'd manage to botch it. He laughed bitterly. King Sarcowicz, general all-around fuck-up. Couldn't even be trusted with his own suicide.

If it had been only Gregory who'd died, he could go to the police and tell them how it happened. It was an accident, just a stupid accident; the window had slipped out of his grasp—Mimi Hargrove knew how heavy the window was, she'd helped lift it the day before, Mimi could back him up. He'd meant to tell about Gregory; he'd been on the point of telling Dennis when he'd realized his partner was dead too. If it were *just* Gregory, he could tell the truth and everybody would say oh-how-horrible and gossip about it with ghoulish relish for a week or so and then eventually forget it.

But *two* fatal accidents—and within minutes of each other? Uh-uh. Not a chance. The police might even accuse him of murder, for god's sake. They couldn't prove murder, of course . . . could they? But just the accusation alone was enough to do him in. What would happen to Keystone Robotics then? How many contracts would come rolling in if everyone thought Keystone's sole surviving partner was a walking death trap for those who worked with him?

Keystone's sole surviving partner. God in heaven, how was he ever going to run the business without Dennis? In a rush, a new sense of loss swept over him and King started crying, quietly at first but then more noisily, like a child. Eventually he calmed down and sat moaning quietly to himself. His stomach growled.

"Hey buddy—you're not thinkin' of takin' a swim, are you?"

King jerked his head around to see a man wearing Sanitation Department coveralls standing between two garbage trucks, fists on hips and head cocked to one side. King scrambled awkwardly to his feet, strangely embarrassed. "No, I, uh." He swallowed and said, "I was just . . . thinking about something. Thanks for your concern." He reddened and hurried past the sanitation worker, banging his knee against the fender of one of the garbage trucks. The other man watched him skeptically, uncertain whether he'd averted a suicide or not.

Still hurrying, King crossed under the old elevated highway and found a street sign that told him he was on West

Fifty-seventh. Ah. Then that was New Jersey he'd been staring at after all, and it was the Hudson he'd almost thrown himself into. And that rusting hulk he'd passed under had to be the West Side Highway. King's rumbling stomach called his attention to the Madison Coffee Shop on the south side of the street.

Thinking that his face must be tear-streaked, King went into the men's room and washed up. He stared at himself in the mirror. He looked all right; he didn't look at all like a man who'd kill two people before lunch. He went back out and ordered pastrami; it came with the usual cole slaw and potato salad. Meat and vegetables; Dennis would have approved.

Since it was early lunchtime, the place was crowded and King had to share a table with a young man wearing a conservative business suit and a Day-Glo green Mohawk haircut. No one but King seemed to find the combination incongruous. Mohawk ate quietly with neat, small gestures, never lifting his eyes from his plate. King put his age at about twenty, twenty-two.

He polished off his mountain of pastrami and felt better. Then suddenly King, who only an hour earlier had taken flight from contact with other people, now wanted that contact in the worst way. He took a sip of his coffee and said, "I wonder why they can never make this stuff taste as good as it smells."

In a deliberate and put-upon manner, Mohawk laid down his fork, raised his eyes from his plate, and said, "Were you speaking to me?"

"Yep. I was wondering why the coffee—"

"I heard what you said. I don't know why they can't make it taste as good as it smells." With that he picked up his fork, lowered his eyes to his plate, and resumed eating. Conversation ended.

King laughed out loud. He was back among the human race, all right, with all its rudeness and its passion for one-upping the other guy. Mohawk hadn't been a member of the adult world very long and was still trying out those of its privileges that were new to him—such as rebuffing a man of his father's generation. King finished his coffee, said "Nice talking to you," and left.

Out on Fifty-seventh Street again, King's momentary buoyancy deserted him. What was he going to do, what in the *hell* was he going to do? He wasn't going to kill himself, at least not now (it was, however, a possibility he intended to hold in reserve). What was left? Admit all, lose the business, go to prison? Try to convince the police that it was too just an accident?

The thought of that unsettled him enough to start him walking—anywhere, just so long as he was on the move. He couldn't go back to the apartment, not with what he'd left there. He couldn't take a plane to Pittsburgh; that's the first place they'd look for him. Should he run and hide? Should he stay and try to bluff it out? He couldn't just wander the streets forever.

He stopped and looked around to get his bearings, and found he was standing in front of a restaurant—Le Biarritz. King realized the pastrami had merely taken the edge off his appetite; he was still hungry. He went inside and had *Escalopes de veau Casimir* with lots of interesting veggies. Dennis would have been proud of him.

Outside again, King felt a lightening of the spirits which he didn't think was attributable solely to the bottle of white wine he'd consumed with the veal. *Never contemplate suicide on an empty stomach*, he moralized. He had a hankering to top off that marvelous French meal with an old-fashioned Amurrican dessert. A few doors down was the Café 57; he went inside and ordered apple pie with a scoop of vanilla ice cream.

Satisfied at last, King continued his aimless stroll east on Fifty-seventh, relishing being alive in a way that was new to him. How could he have considered giving everything up—including the right to wander wherever he pleased, a free man? (Temporarily, at any rate.) He crossed Broadway, glanced over to the other side of Fifty-seventh, and saw the rear end of a black Cadillac sticking out of the side of a building about ten feet above the sidewalk. That bore investigating.

The Caddy was an old model, fins and whitewalls, and it served as a kind of canopy over the door to the Hard Rock Café. People were gathered outside more or less in a line, waiting to get in. One woman stood out from the crowd; she was over six feet tall, with heavily made-up eyes and a magnificent head of frizzy black hair. And prominently displayed on her neck was . . . a vampire bite?

She was talking to some friends when she spotted King. "I don't believe it—somebody taller'n me? Come here, man."

King went there.

She looked him up and down with approval. "Well, well. Where have I been all your life?"

"A meeting of the giants," one of her friends laughed.

"Watch your mouth, you," she scolded. To King she said, "I'm Shawna. What's your name?"

"King."

"I meant your first name."

"King."

"King King?"

"King Sarcowicz."

"Um, we'll stick to King." She noticed him staring at the two bite-sized black dots on her neck and tilted her head to give him a better view. "You like my tattoo?"

"It's . . . different."

"Naw, lotsa people gottum. Beats a butterfly on the ass any day."

"You're advertising yourself as a victim," one of her friends grumbled, a woman.

"Shawna?" another friend scoffed, a man. "No sensible vampire would *dare*."

"Here we go," Shawna growled. "Do I threaten you? I hope?"

King stood listening to their banter and realized he was enjoying himself. He'd taken an instant liking to Shawna; he liked her height and her theatrical looks and her tough way of talking. He decided he even liked her Dracula-was-here tattoo.

Somebody's stomach growled. "Doesn't that line ever move? What time is it?"

Watches were consulted. "Two-thirty," said three voices, one of them King's.

"Two-thirty!" he repeated, aghast. Warren Osterman had called a meeting at MechoTech for two o'clock. That meant that by now . . .

"You're supposed to be someplace," Shawna said accusingly.

"Uh, yes, I am." The thought of what must be going on right then disconcerted him so much that all he could do was stutter. "I, uh, I c-can't, I-I have to, uh—"

"Hey, if it rattles you that much, maybe you'd better not go."

"I can't stay here," he blurted and turned to go—but found the tail of his jacket grasped firmly in Shawna's hand.

"Man, you don't just walk away like that. Where's your manners? Doncha have a card or a phone number or somethin'?"

"Oh. Yes, yes I do." He fumbled a Keystone Robotics business card out of his billfold and Shawna released his jacket to take it. King was afraid he was going to break down right there in front of them. "I'm sorry, Shawna." He turned and darted into the traffic.

There was a screech of brakes followed by the sound of a cab driver's colorful profanity. Safely on the other side of the street, King heard Shawna call: "Pittsburgh?"

King stumbled on for a block and crossed Seventh Avenue. He stopped in front of a playbill mounted in a glass case; he stared at it without seeing what it said, needing a moment to get a grip on himself. What was happening right then? When nobody showed up at the meeting, Warren Osterman must have—wait a minute, what about Mimi Hargrove? She'd spent the night at the airport hotel, and King didn't know whether she'd been planning to come back to the apartment first or go straight to the meeting at MechoTech. If she'd gone back to the apartment, that meant she was the one who'd found Dennis and Gregory . . . *Oh, god, Mimi, I'm sorry!* It was the first time he'd thought of what it would be like to walk in and find a headless body in the living room and an electrocuted one in the bathtub.

But if Mimi had not gone back to the apartment first . . . then maybe no one knew about it yet. They'd know soon enough, though, when only Mimi showed up for the meeting. And the only one of the four staying at the apartment who was missing was King Sarcowicz. If they weren't looking for him already, it was only a matter of time until they were.

King became aware that the placard in the glass case he was staring at wasn't a playbill at all, technically; it was a listing of concerts scheduled to take place. To his surprise he found he was standing in front of Carnegie Hall. Well, not exactly the front. He walked around the corner to Seventh Avenue where the stage entrance was located . . .

. . . and experienced an overwhelming sense of loss. King had never been to a concert at Carnegie Hall. It was one of those things he'd always assumed he'd get around to doing one of these days, sometime soon in a pleasantly vague future that stretched on forever. But now he might never have the chance. That started him thinking of all the other things he'd never get to do. He'd never ride the Trans-Siberian Railroad. He'd never go looking for the Loch Ness monster.

More importantly, he'd never get a chance to realize the dreams he'd had for years—dreams about things that were no longer possible only in the distant future but coming closer every day. Such as insectlike robots that could climb vertical surfaces, that could clean and do maintenance work on the outsides of buildings. He'd never get to build one of those spiderbots. And he'd never design the first fully automated airplane . . . oh, why stop there? He'd never work on the first intelligent starship. All those opportunities that used to lie ahead of him—gone.

King gave himself a little shake; this was no time to indulge in a sentimental longing for things he'd never know. He went back to Fifty-seventh, which he was beginning to think of as "his" street. Close to Carnegie Hall was the Verve Naturelle Restaurant; more to break his peculiar mood than for any other reason he went in and ordered something called a Powerhouse, which turned out to be orange juice, ice cream, and honey, with a little protein powder mixed in. Next he came to the Russian Tea Room. As if on automatic drive, he headed inside.

In midafternoon the restaurant wasn't too crowded. King was seated in a low central booth that made him feel terribly exposed. But he forgot about being conspicuous as soon as the chicken Kiev arrived. Delicious! He managed to spill his wine before he was through; a sad-eyed Polish waiter gave him a tragic look but said nothing. King left an extra-big tip.

It wasn't until he was pounding the sidewalk again that he began to wonder where this ravenous appetite of his had come from. He'd never eaten so much before at one time in his life. And he didn't feel sick, or even bloated. Just one more strange thing on this strangest of days. It was the only time he'd killed, and it was the only time he'd stuffed himself like a pig. What was the connection?

Speaking of eating... *Why, look what's here,* King thought. An eatery named O'Neals—just what he needed. For the second time that afternoon he topped off a sumptuous meal with pie à la mode. Cherry pie, this time.

King was getting up to leave when a boy of twelve or thirteen came in and sat down. Wide-eyed, the boy looked up at King's six-foot-ten and said, "Wow, you must be a—"

"No, I'm not," King answered shortly and turned to go.

"Why not?"

That stopped him. In all his years of explaining that he was not now nor had never been a professional basketball player, no one had ever asked him why. He looked at the boy skeptically. "You really want to know, kid?"

"Yeah, I wanna know." Defiantly.

"Okay." King sat down next to him. "In the first place, I'm too old to play now. I'm forty-five."

"But when you were younger—"

"When I was younger, I was nothing less than a mobile disaster-area on the court. I tried. I really did try. The basketball coach in high school saw me walking down a corridor one day and practically dragged me to the gym. But he couldn't teach me to play. You see, I've always been poorly coordinated—it's a physical problem. I kept tripping over my own feet, knocking down my teammates, fouling the other guys. Finally the coach just positioned me under the basket and told me not to move at all—just wait for the other players to feed me the ball."

King paused while the boy ordered something to eat. "Did it work?" the youngster wanted to know.

"No way. I couldn't manage even that. I fouled out of every game I was in—usually in the first quarter. Finally the coach let me go. He said in time I'd grow out of it."

"Didja?"

"Nope. The same thing happened in college. It's too bad, in a way. I like basketball." It was the only sport he did like.

"So do I," the boy said, tugging at his tie and grimacing. "That's too bad, mister."

"My name's King. What's yours?"

"Ricky." He pulled at his tie again.

"Why are you so dressed up on a school day?"

"Aw, my mom always makes me wear a tie when we go see the lawyer. There are all these problems about settling my dad's estate and we have to keep goin' back alla time."

His dad's *estate*. "I'm sorry, Ricky," King said, meaning it. "Did your dad die recently?"

"November."

"And there's trouble with the will?"

"Naw, something about the trust funds, I dunno. That's what Mr. Liebermann says."

"Liebermann—that's the lawyer?"

"Howard J. M. Liebermann the Great."

"Two middle initials?"

"Yeah, one's not enough for him, I guess. You know what I think? I don't think there's any legal problem at all. I think Liebermann's just gettin' it off with my mom."

Mildly shocked, King asked, "What makes you think that?"

"You think I'm stupid or somethin'? I can tell." Ricky squirmed in his seat. "He's married."

King's first impulse was to tell Ricky he must be mistaken. But the kid looked so *sure*—and whether he was right or wrong, it wouldn't do to dismiss his fears as foolishness. King thought a few moments and said, "Your mom must be feeling pretty alone and frightened right now, and she knows your dad isn't ever coming back to make it right. Who knows why these things happen? Maybe Liebermann just said the right thing at the right time."

"But what do I do?"

"Well, first of all you don't put pressure on her. Let her know you love her. Look for things you and your mom can do together—look hard, Ricky. It's got to be the two of you together from now on, you know."

Just then Ricky's order arrived, an elaborate gooey dessert that only a thirteen-year-old could love. Eagerly he dug in.

King stood up. "Your mom will be all right, Ricky. Just be patient."

Ricky grinned at him around a mouthful of whipped cream. "Thanks, Mr. King."

King waved acknowledgment and left the restaurant. Resuming his eastward trek, he mused over the role-reversal going on between Ricky and his mom and wondered how common that was in families in which one of the parents died. Then it suddenly hit him: he, King-of-the-Fuck-Ups Sarcowicz, master of *gaucherie* and botcher of friendships, unintentional killer of his fellow man—*he* had been giving personal advice! King let loose a sharp, hysterical laugh and failed to notice the crowd parting around him. He carefully thought over the scene in O'Neals and finally concluded he hadn't said anything that could hurt the boy.

On he plodded toward the East River, past Marlborough Gallery, Tiffany, another art gallery. Victoria's Secret. A man carrying a cello and another struggling with an oversized painting did a funny little dance to avoid crashing into each other. King did crash into a high-punk male of indeterminate age, apologized, and got called a muh'fuh for his trouble.

He spotted the Mitsukoshi Restaurant on the northeast corner of Fifty-seventh and Park. King crossed over and mingled with the crowd at the sushi bar, frankly surprised to find that raw fish was still so popular. When he came out he decided he wanted some more fish, but cooked this time. Back across the street to Bruce Ho's Four Seas Restaurant, where he was served flounder stuffed with crabmeat and spicy little shrimp.

A few doors farther down he came to Tommy Makem's Irish Pavilion; King went in and asked for cheesecake but declined the Irish coffee.

Though there was still some daylight left, the afternoon was easing into early evening. The first of the dinner crowd were beginning the hunt for their evening meal; King passed up Mr. Chow's because the place was already getting crowded. In the next block he went into Tony Roma's and ordered ribs. But then before he was finished, he paused with a rib halfway to his mouth: he couldn't eat another bite. Not even one; his ravenous appetite had at last been satisfied. He put the rib down.

With satisfaction came fatigue; his feet were beginning to hurt as well. King left Tony Roma's and automatically headed east, having nowhere else to go. Then suddenly there it was: the East River—his afternoon-long, pointless goal. King acknowledged wryly he'd no more be able to throw himself into those greasy waters than he'd been able to jump into the Hudson.

He was in Sutton Place, one of the good places to live in New York. He walked into a pleasant little park distinguished by the unexpected presence of a bronze statue of a pig. A rather courtly-looking elderly man was sitting on a bench, leaning his weight on the cane he held in front of him. King sat down on the other end of the bench—and belched. "Whoops. Excuse me."

The old man nodded agreeably in his direction. "Something you ate."

"I wouldn't be at all surprised," King laughed. "I just ate my way across Fifty-seventh Street."

"A lot of good restaurants on Fifty-seventh," the old man remarked, "and a nice choice of foods."

It had been a day of restaurants and food. "Food is sustenance," King muttered to himself, "and I have been sustaining myself. That's what I was doing."

"Of course, Le Pavillon is gone now," the old man went on. "But I hope you treated yourself to a feast at the Parker Meridien."

"The what?"

"The dining room of the Hotel Parker Meridien—one of the best in the city, I've always thought. Do you know it? It's between Sixth and Seventh."

Between O'Neals and the Russian Tea Room. "I missed it," King said, disappointed.

"Well. The next time you're in town."

King looked at him sharply. "How did you know I was from out of town?"

The old man lifted one frail shoulder, let it drop. "You don't walk like a New Yorker."

Thinking that at this point he probably wasn't walking like a Pennsylvanian either, King stretched out his tired legs and aching feet and closed his eyes. The day was catching up with him. On the brink of nodding off, he jerked himself awake; he ought to be thinking about finding a place to hole up for the night. The trouble was, he was almost out of money. He'd used credit cards wherever he could in his omnivorous journey across Fifty-seventh, but he always liked to leave the tip in cash. He roused himself enough to ask his bench partner, "Do you know if there's a bank machine near here?"

To King's surprise, the old man leaned forward and spat angrily upon the ground. "Machines! No, I don't know where you can find a bank machine. I never use them."

"Why not? It beats standing in line inside the bank."

"So instead you stand in line *out*side the bank. And get wet when it rains. Besides, the blasted machines don't work half the time . . . none of them do, not any kind of machine." The old man sniffed loudly. "Machines to do this, machines to do that. We even depend on machines to do our thinking for us now. Camus was right. Man's greatest desire is to be a stone in the road. He wouldn't have to think for himself, he wouldn't have to make intelligent choices—all he'd have to do is lie there, like the lump that he is."

King was simply too tired to appreciate having Camus quoted at him just then. Besides, he'd run into technophobes before; there was no arguing with them. Wearily he hauled himself to his feet and said, "Nevertheless, I need some cash and the banks are closed. I have to find a machine."

"Suit yourself," the old man answered, and closed his face.

King automatically headed back the way he'd come—but then he stopped. Fifty-seventh Street had been a blessing, offering as it did a numbing, anaesthetic effect to help him through those first terrible hours after Dennis and Gregory had died. But now the anaesthesia was wearing off, and he didn't want to go back. Abruptly he turned right and headed uptown.

And found that the same thing happened in New York that happened in Pittsburgh: every time he needed a bank machine, somebody went out and hid them all. Up the short blocks, across the long blocks . . . King tramped back and forth for forty minutes before he found a machine willing to disgorge a little out-of-town money. After a slight delay, the machine reluctantly let him have two hundred of his own dollars. He let the bank receipt—which wasn't really a receipt—flutter down to the sidewalk where it joined thirty or forty others, all waiting to be swept up the following morning by a grumbling bank employee.

King's feet were really hurting now. Up ahead was Central Park; he'd sit down and try to figure out what to do next. He crossed Central Park South, glancing longingly over his shoulder at the hotels beckoning from the south side of the street; there was the St. Moritz, and Essex House. King wanted nothing more than a tub to soak his feet in and a comfortable bed to lie on—but wouldn't the police be checking the hotels for him? Not that he'd register under his own name, of course, but he'd still be easy to identify. People tended to remember a man who was nearly seven feet tall. This needed thinking out.

There was still enough light that King wasn't worried about getting caught in the park after dark. He was tempted just to stretch out on the grass instead of looking for a place to sit down; but nobody else in sight was recumbent and King was afraid of calling attention to himself. Finally he spotted a park bench, the old-fashioned kind with iron armrests, and it was empty. He hurried his step.

He almost made it. Just before he reached the bench, four boys suddenly stepped out of nowhere to block his path. "Hoo-ee, looka the basketball player!" one of them hooted.

"I'm not a basketball player," King said and tried to pass.

The boys closed ranks. "Where you think you goin', Shorty?"

King looked at them more carefully. They were Hispanic kids, the youngest not much older than the boy Ricky, fourteen or fifteen at the most. All four were dressed in jeans and sneakers and identical green windbreakers. King felt a little flutter in his stomach as he said, "I'm going to that bench. I'm tired and my feet hurt and I want to sit down." *Mistake!* his mind shrieked as soon as he'd said it. *Don't show them your weak spots!*

The one who seemed to be the leader laughed unpleasantly. "But that's our bench. Dincha know that was our bench? And nobody sits on our bench without payin' for the pri-vi-lege." He stretched the last word out insolently. *"No-bod-y.* Got that, Shorty? Ya wanna sit, ya gotta pay."

If King hadn't been so tired, he would have turned and walked away right then. As it was, he thought it better just to pay up and be done with this nonsense. "How much?"

"A *thousssand* dollars an hour," the leader hissed.

"A thousand—" King broke off his protest when he saw the boys circling him. How could young boys be so menacing? Without saying a word they backed him up toward the bench. A knife had appeared in the leader's hand, and one of the others was swinging a sock filled with . . . coins? Lead pellets? "But it's still daylight!" King cried out stupidly, outraged by this breach of mugging decorum.

Suddenly his legs buckled; one of the boys had kicked him behind the knees. As his head bobbed down to their level, he saw the weighed sock swinging toward his face. Too late, he tried to throw up his arms to protect himself. Pain like he'd never felt before shot through his cheek, his eye, his upper lip—and down he went, striking his head against the iron armrest of the park bench as he fell.

And King Sarcowicz felt nothing more at all for a long, long time.

* 6 *

The next time King opened his eyes, it was to see a Hispanic face peering closely at him. But this one was a woman's face, middle-aged; and it looked concerned. She was a nurse, and King was in a hospital.

"Ah, you're coming round," the nurse said in a tone of satisfaction. "Can you talk? How do you feel?"

"Lousy," King said through a mouth that felt stuffed full of cotton. "Uh can't talk."

She nodded. "You have a mild concussion, and," she made a face, "you're going to have one hell of a shiner. Here—take some ice water. It'll clear out your mouth.

King sucked greedily at the tube in the glass she held out to him. It did make his mouth feel better. Carefully, he eased himself up to a sitting position. "Whoo. I don't remember coming here."

"You were still unconscious when you were brought in. Whatever hit you, it loosened a couple of your teeth—you'll have to see a dentist after you're discharged. But Dr. Fabrizio will explain all that to you. He'll be in later."

He reached up and touched a bandage on his left cheek.

"Minor lacerations," the nurse explained. "No stitches were required. And no bones were broken—you were lucky."

Oh, really? "Why don't I feel lucky?" King grumbled.

"It could have been a lot worse," she said briskly. "How's your memory? Do you know who you are?"

He blinked at her. "Of course I know who I am."

"Good. A lot of concussed patients experience confusion and disorientation when they first regain consciousness. See, I told you you were lucky! Now, I need your name and address for our records. You didn't have any identification on you."

King told her his name and where he was staying in New York. "No billfold?"

She shook her head. "The mugger must have taken it."

"More than one. Four of them."

"Four! No wonder you didn't have a chance. Mr. Sarcowicz, a couple of police officers are waiting to talk to you. Are you up to seeing them?"

Police! God, there was no running and hiding now. But surely they were here about the mugging? "I'll see them."

The nurse was almost out the door when he called out, "Oh—excuse me? I'm sorry, I don't know your name."

"I'm Mrs. Sanchez."

"Mrs. Sanchez, would you make a telephone call for me? Please call Warren Osterman at MechoTech Corporation. The number is . . ." King waved a hand vaguely. "His card's in my billfold."

Her eyebrow went up a fraction. "Your billfold was stolen," she reminded him gently.

"Oh." He wasn't as clear-headed as he'd thought. "Well, the number's in the book, under MechoTech. Tell him . . . tell him I'm sorry."

"Sorry for what?"

King barked a short laugh, sending a new pain shooting through his head. "Tell him I'm sorry I missed the meeting."

"Oh, I think he'll understand," she smiled. "But you can call him yourself if you're feeling up to it." She pointed to the telephone on the stand between King's bed and the one next to it. "There's a directory in the drawer. Do you still want me to make the call?"

"Ah—no, no thank you. I didn't see the phone."

Mrs. Sanchez nodded and left. King looked around him. There were ten beds in the hospital room, all occupied; King's was next to the wall by the door, farthest from the room's one window. In the bed next to his lay a man in his sixties, his eyes closed and a tube running up his nose.

Mrs. Sanchez was back, followed by two uniformed police officers. One of the policemen was big and black, and the other was small and Oriental—*stereotypes on parade*, King thought. They introduced themselves as Officers Jones and O'Leary; O'Leary was the Oriental. Jones did most of the talking. He wanted King's name and address and then a quick summary of what had happened.

"I was mugged in the park," King said helplessly. "What else can I tell you? They took my billfold." He glanced at his naked left wrist. "And my watch."

"How much cash?" Jones asked.

"Two hundred in new twenties. I'd just been to a bank machine."

"Credit cards?"

"Seven or eight. Seven."

"American Express? Visa?"

"Both." King went on to name the rest.

"You have the account numbers written down somewhere?"

"My partner does. He takes care of that sort of thing." Then King realized what he'd just said. *Oh, Dennis.*

"You all right?"

"Uh—yes, I'm all right."

"You turned pale there for a second."

"I'm all right," King repeated. "Officer Jones, how did I get here? The last thing I remember was one of them swinging a sock full of something heavy at my face."

"They whacked you from the back too," Jones said, "Or else you hit your head on something when you fell. They must have thought they'd killed you, 'cause they dragged you behind some shrubbery. A woman came along later and saw one of your feet sticking out and called us. You could have been there for hours."

For hours? Something clicked in King's traumatized brain. Were those kid hoodlums going to give him an alibi? "What time is it?"

The Oriental named O'Leary looked at his wrist. "Five to ten. We got the call at seven-fifteen. What time were you attacked, Mr. Sarcowicz?"

King swallowed. "I . . . I'm not sure."

Jones said, "Mr. Sarcowicz, I know you're feeling rotten but anything you can remember might help. What time did you go into the park?"

"I really don't know, Officer. I'd been wandering around the streets and my feet were starting to hurt. I just wanted to sit down for a while." That much was true.

"When was this? Before lunch? After?"

King swallowed and decided to take the plunge. "Before. I had a meeting at two—which I didn't make."

"Before," Jones repeated. "How much before? Were you getting hungry?"

"Yes," King said eagerly, grabbing at the lifeline. "I was beginning to get hungry."

"Around noon, then?"

"That sounds about right." King swallowed, scared to death they'd see through the lie.

O'Leary spoke up. "How many of them were there, Mr. Sarcowicz?"

"Four."

"Can you describe them?"

"They were kids! All four of them! I was mugged by a bunch of schoolboys."

Jones's face crinkled into a sad smile. "I doubt if those boys spent much time in school. Were they black? Hispanic?"

King was about to say Hispanic when he shot a glance at Mrs. Sanchez, doing something for the patient in the next bed. Then he looked back at Jones's black face and O'Leary's Oriental one. "White," he said. "They were white."

O'Leary pressed for specifics, so King made up two descriptions and said he didn't remember the other two very well. King watched O'Leary writing in a notebook and thought about his junior muggers; they were welcome to the cash and the watch and the credit cards if those four were going to keep him out of prison—he hoped the police never caught them. Jones told him they'd want him to come in and look at mug shots when he was feeling better.

There was no way King was going to identify four kids who could give it away that he'd been lying about the time he was mugged, but he told the policemen he'd be in. "What are the chances of catching them, Officer?"

"If you can pick their pictures out of the book, the chances are pretty good. But that two hundred bucks has already been spent—make up your mind to that. And get your partner to report the stolen credit cards right away. Don't wait."

"I'll do it tonight."

The two police officers left. *They believed me! God Almighty, they believed me!* King covered his face with his hands to hide his exhilaration.

"Are you all right, Mr. Sarcowicz?"

King lowered his hands. "I'm just fine, Mrs. Sanchez." She went about her business while King lay there enjoying the first real feeling of relief he'd had all day.

That lasted about five minutes. Then it gradually sank in on him that all he'd done was provide himself with an alibi from noon on. The medical examination would show Dennis and Gregory had died several hours before that, wouldn't it?

God in heaven, what was the matter with him? Why hadn't he said he was mugged at nine or ten in the morning? The police wouldn't know any different, since the four thuglings had so considerately hidden him in the bushes. But perhaps the medical evidence wouldn't be able to pinpoint the time of death that exactly—was that possible? If it couldn't, then he still had a chance of getting out of this.

A *chance*. It was still unsettled, still up in the air. He'd had the opportunity to clear himself once and for all—and he blew it. Naturally.

That one last bit of evidence of his own ineptitude proved to be the final straw. All the traumas of the day ganged up on King and knocked him out. He fell into a deep, dream-filled sleep that lasted for eleven hours.

Wednesday he'd arrived in New York and had the design job of his life land in his lap. Thursday he'd accidentally killed two colleagues, spent the day eating, and gotten mugged. Friday the doctor told him he could probably go home later in the day—if he stayed in bed most of the time, rested, took it easy, and came back for a check-up on Monday. King promised to do all those things.

Now he lay in the hospital bed with the phone directory open to MechoTech. He couldn't put off calling Warren Osterman any longer, but he was having trouble cranking himself up for the task. King was going to have to play the injured innocent, the brutally beaten victim of a vicious gang of hardened criminals—flat on his back, helpless, and with no idea that Dennis Cox and Gregory Dillard were dead. That was a hell of a lot to bring off.

He'd just pulled the telephone over into his lap when the door opened and two women came in. One, a nurse, pointed to his bed and left. The other, a nondescript sort of person it would be easy to forget, came over to him and held up a gold shield.

"I'm Detective Sergeant Larch of the NYPD," the woman said. "You are King Sarcowicz?"

A police detective? King swallowed and said, "I am. I told the two officers who were here last night all I could about the muggers."

"That's not what I'm here about, Mr. Sarcowicz. May I sit down?" Without waiting for an answer she pulled a chair up beside his bed. "You're one of the owners of Keystone Robotics in Pittsburgh? In partnership with Dennis Cox?"

King's heart pounded. "Yes."

"Could you tell me when you last saw Mr. Cox?"

"Yesterday morning. Why?"

"What time was that?"

Careful. "Uh, I don't know exactly. Fairly early."

"You left the apartment early? How early?"

King's skin began to itch. "I didn't check the time, Sergeant. What's this all about?"

"Before nine, after nine?"

"Around nine, I guess it was—maybe ten. Sergeant . . . ?"

"Larch, Sergeant Marian Larch. Where was Mr. Cox when you left?"

"In the bathtub, soaking. He has a bad back."

"And Gregory Dillard? Where was he?"

"Gregory? He was still in the apartment when I left." King's skin was itching furiously; the police suspected him! Already, they suspected him! *Admit nothing. Volunteer nothing.* "Sergeant Larch, why are you asking me these questions? What's going on?"

Sergeant Larch took a deep breath and said, "I'm afraid I have bad news for you, Mr. Sarcowicz. It's about your partner."

"Something's happened to Dennis?"

"Yes, sir. I'm sorry to tell you this, but he's dead."

King had no difficulty in looking shocked. Hearing the words spoken aloud by another person brought it all home again. He closed his eyes and saw again the little red TV set in the bathwater between Dennis's legs. He saw Dennis's perfectly still body, his open eyes. King opened his own eyes and looked at the police detective watching him sympathetically. What would she expect him to say? "How?" he croaked.

"He was electrocuted, in the bath. There was a small television set in the water with him."

"Oh, no!" King gave a sincere-sounding groan. "I warned him about that! I told him it was dangerous to use small appliances where they could fall into the water! Oh, my god—Dennis!"

Sergeant Larch waited a moment and said, "I'm afraid there's something more." Then she told him about Gregory Dillard.

King threw both arms up over his face. He was going to have to do some acting now; he couldn't get as worked up over Gregory as over Dennis. Still keeping his face covered, he cried out, "That goddam heavy window! It took two of us to lift it the day before! Why did he try it by himself?"

"Well, sir, we're not sure he did. Look, I can see you're upset—we'll finish this later. Do you know when you're getting out of the hospital?"

"Possibly later today—the doctor is waiting for some test results. What do you mean, you're not sure Gregory tried to lift the window alone?"

She took a deep breath. "Mr. Sarcowicz, when three out of four people staying in the same apartment are all victims of violence on the same day, wouldn't you wonder what was going on? Isn't it possible that it might have been four out of four if Mimi Hargrove hadn't spent the night somewhere else?"

"You think the mugging . . . ?"

"May not have been a mugging. We've had an APB out on you for twenty-four hours, Mr. Sarcowicz—we didn't know what had become of you. My partner just happened to see your name on a printout of crimes reported last night or else I wouldn't be here now. Did you let anybody know what had happened?"

Think fast. King pointed to the telephone resting in his lap. "I just now left a message for Warren Osterman at MechoTech."

"Warren Osterman? Didn't you try to call your partner?"

King's mouth went dry. "It's nearly eleven. I thought everybody'd be at MechoTech."

Sergeant Marian Larch accepted that, and said she'd talk to him again later. She expressed her sympathy for his loss in a way that made him believe she meant it, and then she left.

King called Warren Osterman as fast as his finger could punch out the number.

It was four in the afternoon before King's doctor told him he could go, repeating his warnings about bed rest and coming back for a check-up. In a way, King didn't want to leave the hospital; he felt safe there. Outside, there would be questions.

Warren Osterman couldn't come himself, so he sent Rae Borchard, she of the enigmatic persona. "There's no question of your staying in that apartment now," she said briskly. "Warren wants you moved to another apartment we maintain for out-of-town visitors. Mrs. Hargrove is there already."

"I'll need to pick up my things."

"Yes. We'll make it as fast as possible."

King cleared his throat. "Do you know if the, uh, what I mean is . . . ?"

"The bodies have been removed."

MechoTech took care of the hospital bill. Rae Borchard drove a Mercedes 560 SL, the same model as Dennis's. On the way to the first apartment, she did her best to assure King that he'd be safe in the new building. "Six security guards are on duty around the clock. In addition, there's a state-of-the-art alarm system that's connected to the police precinct house. There won't be anyone slipping uninvited into *that* apartment."

"You think Mimi and I are in danger?"

"Warren Osterman thinks so. There's a lot of money riding on our project. Warren's convinced some competitor is out to kill off the entire design team, to force MechoTech to default on the contract."

Now there was a novel idea. "*Warren's* convinced. You're not?"

She paused, considering her answer. "I think it's possible, of course. But not very probable, frankly. Still, there's no point in taking chances. Warren will want to talk to you about security. But for the time being, please just stay in the apartment, Mr. Sarcowicz."

"Call me King. Please."

"I'll be happy to, King. And you call me Rae."

That sounded friendly. "Rae, a police detective who came to the hospital hinted at the same thing Warren's afraid of—a Sergeant Marian Larch?"

"Sergeant Larch, yes. I've spoken to her."

"She intimated the only reason Mimi is alive is that she spent the night with her husband at the airport hotel. She seems to think my mugging wasn't really a mugging, but an attempt at murder." Sergeant Larch had not, in fact, been anywhere near that positive about it, but King rather liked being cast as the victim who escaped. "Oh—I just remembered something. The police officers who found me said the 'muggers' hid me behind some shrubbery because they thought they'd killed me. I don't remember anything about that. I was unconscious at the time."

Rae was silent for a few moments. Then she said: "They thought they'd killed you? That changes things." She shot him an anguished look. "Maybe Warren's right after all."

King fingered the bandage on his face. That was the first time Rae Borchard had shown anything of what she was feeling. King felt a prick of guilt for the worry he was causing her—and Warren Osterman as well. But if everyone wanted to think he was the intended victim of some industrial conspiracy that had already disposed of Dennis and Gregory . . .

"The police are still here." Rae pulled up to the building from which King had fled in such panic the day before; she left the Mercedes in a no-parking area right behind a black-and-white prowl car. "I hope they don't hold us up."

"I'm supposed to go straight to bed," King said. "We can use that as an excuse."

Upstairs, King's heart started pounding as they approached the apartment. How should he act? Uneasy, frightened, depressed? He thought he could probably manage all three without even breathing hard. Rae unlocked the door—to find Sergeant Marian Larch on the other side.

"You have your own key, Ms Borchard?" the policewoman asked pointedly.

"Unused keys are kept at the MechoTech offices," Rae replied coolly. "I checked one out this afteroon. Sergeant Larch, Mr. Sarcowicz needs to collect his personal belongings. Then we'll be out of your way."

"Will he be saying at the same apartment you've moved Mrs. Hargrove to?"

I'm right here, King thought; *ask me.*

"That's right," Rae answered. "So, if we may come in . . . ?"

Marian Larch moved aside to let them enter. "How are you feeling, Mr. Sarcowicz?"

"Shaky, but okay, considering. I'm supposed to go to bed."

Three or four men were prowling about the apartment looking for . . . what? Sergeant Larch gestured to one of them to come over, a man of about her own age, somewhere in the indeterminate thirties. "Ivan, this is King Sarcowicz," she said. "Mr. Sarcowicz, this is my partner, Sergeant Malecki."

Sergeant Malecki's face lit up as he looked at King. "Say, didn't you used to play for the Knicks?"

King sighed. "No, that was someone else."

"The Celtics, then—yeah, it was the Celtics!"

"It wasn't anybody. I've never been a basketball player."

Malecki looked disappointed. "Too bad. Well, as long as you're here, answer one question for me. What do you know about a one-footed pigeon?"

Of all the questions he could have asked, that was the last King would have expected. He told the police about the lame bird and her mate that Gregory Dillard had fed bagel crumbs to on Wednesday. "Is that what he was doing when he died?" *Look innocent.*

"Mimi Hargrove thinks so. What other reason could he have for leaning out the window?"

"None that I can think of."

"Oh, by the way, there's been a woman telephoning this apartment for you. Name of Gale Fredericks?"

King nodded. "My assistant, in Pittsburgh. I'll call her later."

Rae Borchard waited in the living room while King went to his bedroom to pack. When he had all his clothes in his suitcase, he realized he'd left his shaver in the bathroom. In *the* bathroom. He hesitated, but then chided himself for being foolish. It was just a bathroom.

Once in the bathroom, however, he couldn't bring himself to look at the tub. When he'd found his shaver, he glanced up at his reflection in the mirror. He needed a shave, but that was the least of his problems; he looked as if he'd gone fifteen rounds with Godzilla and lost every one. The bandage on his cheek failed to conceal an ugly purplish-blue bruise that covered the entire left side of his face. The area around his eye was swollen as well as discolored; King wouldn't make the cover of *Hunk* this month. Gingerly he touched his tongue against his upper left cuspid and one of the bicuspids and felt both teeth move.

Back in his bedroom he tossed the shaver into the suitcase and took one last look around. The specifications and summaries and other papers Rae Borchard had distributed—he'd need them. He zipped up his suitcase and carried it into the office. King's face and head were beginning to hurt again; he'd been handed a vial of pain pills at the hospital, but he wasn't to take any more until six o'clock. He glanced at his wrist, remembering too late he no longer had a watch.

As quickly as he could, he gathered up his papers and was on the verge of leaving when he remembered the sketches of the gun platform he'd put into the computer. He turned on the machine he'd used and called up the file containing his preliminary designs. *Oh, shit.* King felt a big letdown when he looked at the results of that first eager burst of creative activity. There was nothing there he could use; the designs were more reflective of boyish enthusiasm than of any insight into a highly specialized design problem. He'd done this before, started out with a wild flurry of half-formulated ideas that later had to be scrapped. *You'd think I'd know better by now,* he thought. With three keystrokes he erased the contents of the file.

He was trying to figure out how to juggle all his papers and carry a suitcase at the same time when Sergeant Marian Larch walked into the room. "Mr. Sarcowicz, one question before you go. Had you been using the computers yesterday morning right before you left the apartment?"

"No. Why?"

"When we got here, all three machines were turned on. Nothing showing on the screens, but they were on."

"Strange." Then it hit him: in his stupor after realizing he'd killed Dennis as well as Gregory, he'd wandered in here and powered up all three machines for no reason other than to be doing something. But he couldn't tell Sergeant Larch *that*. "Maybe Gregory was using them."

"All three of them? Is that usual?"

"No, it's not," King admitted.

"What's in those computers?"

"Just various software programs. That middle one has a CAD program—"

"Excuse me—a what?"

"A computer-aided design program. I used it Wednesday night to work out some preliminary sketches I'd made."

"Sketches of what?" Marian Larch asked. "This gun platform you're all working on?"

"That's right." King's mind was working furiously; was this something he could use? "I'm glad you reminded me, Sergeant. I almost went away and left them here." He dumped his armload of papers on the table and powered up the same computer he'd just turned off a minute ago. "That's odd," he said when the file showed up empty.

"What's odd?" Sergeant Larch asked.

"Wait a minute." King went through a ritual of searching for the nonexistent sketches. "I don't understand. I'm sure I saved those designs."

"You're telling me they're missing?"

"Well, there's the file I stored them in. And you can see it's empty."

"Somebody stole them? Can that be done?"

"Easily. All you have to do is copy the file to a floppy and then erase the original."

"Could you have erased the designs by accident?"

King pretended to think. "No, the way this program's set up—if I had erased anything accidentally, the whole file would be gone. But the *file* is here. Only the contents are gone."

Sergeant Larch nodded, thinking. "Yet the thief left all these papers here." She gestured toward the table where King had dumped them. "They were right there when we got here. Isn't any of that stuff classified?"

"I don't think so. Rae Borchard could tell you." King decided a little protest was in order. "Sergeant, these were only preliminary sketches that were stolen. They wouldn't be of any help to anybody."

"Maybe the thief didn't know that. Let's go talk to Rae Borchard." She picked up King's suitcase and left him to gather up his papers still one more time. He followed her into the living room, where she was telling her partner and Rae Borchard that King's designs had been stolen out of the computer. Sergeant Larch pointed out that a whole mess of interesting-looking papers had been left behind and asked if they contained classified material.

"No, there's nothing especially confidential about those papers," Rae answered when asked. "Mostly they're details of the earlier design teams' failures—"

"Wait a minute," Sergeant Ivan Malecki interrupted. "What earlier design teams?"

Rae explained how the Defense Department had been trying for years to develop a reliable high-tech weapons platform. "The platform specifications are classified, of course. But they are known to the four other firms who'd earlier tried and failed."

Sergeant Malecki wanted to make sure he had that clear. "You're saying that those papers are old news to everybody who had a go at it before you?"

"Yes."

Malecki glanced at his partner. "That narrows it down."

She nodded and said to Rae Borchard, "Can you give us a list of the earlier designers?"

"Certainly. You think it was one of them who's behind this?"

Marian Larch gave a noncommittal shrug. "It's the only lead we've got."

Slowly Rae Borchard turned and looked at King, her expression one of concern.

The two sergeants noticed. "Yeah, he's still in danger," Malecki said, "if we got this figured right. Mr. Sarcowicz, that new apartment building you're going to is like a fortress. We checked it out, and we couldn't give you better protection ourselves. Just stay inside until we get a chance to nail whoever killed your partner and Mr. Dillard. Y'unnerstand?"

"I understand," King croaked, his forehead wet with sweat.

"We'll be along to talk to you later," Sergeant Larch added. "Right now you'd better get back to bed. You're not looking any too steady."

"Yes, I would like to lie down," King said in his most plaintive tone.

Immediately Rae Borchard was on her feet. "Then we'll go right now. Here, let me take the papers."

King handed her his papers and picked up the suitcase. He mumbled something by way of farewell and followed Rae out, relieved to escape the official presence of the two police sergeants.

In Rae's car once again, he started complaining. "I can't stay in the apartment all the time! I have work to do."

"We'll bring the work to you. Do as the police say, King. Stay inside."

"But I have to go out. I need to buy another watch, and I want to get a briefcase."

"I'll have my secretary pick them up. What kind of watch do you want?"

"Just time and date, nothing fancy." He started to reach into his pocket and then remembered. "Oh. My credit cards were stolen."

Rae waved a hand. "We'll take care of it. MechoTech got you into this mess, it's the least we can do. Have you reported the theft to your credit card companies?"

"Not yet. The record of the account numbers is in Pittsburgh. I'll ask Gale Fredericks to see to it."

"The woman who called—your assistant?"

"That's the one."

"Anything else we can do for you here?"

King thought a moment. "Could you recommend a dentist?"

Rae looked a question at him.

King touched his upper lip. "A couple of teeth were knocked loose."

Rae pressed her lips together and concentrated on the traffic. "I'll have an appointment set up for tomorrow."

King thanked her and leaned back and closed his eyes. He felt at ease for the first time since he'd left the hospital. Things were going unbelievably well. What a stroke of luck he'd erased that file from the computer! That had been just the thing to convince the police that a MechoTech competitor was indeed on a murderous mission to win back the Defense contract. Sergeants Larch and Malecki would soon be off on their wild goose chase and out of his hair; his chances were looking better and better.

King still had a little trouble believing he was going to get away with it; things didn't usually fall into place that neatly for him. But if he just kept quiet and didn't try to elaborate on his story, the police shouldn't have any reason to suspect he'd had anything to do with Dennis's and Gregory's deaths. They were looking for a murderer now, and King was not a murderer. Lethally clumsy, but not a murderer.

Murder required an intent to kill, a desire to inflict harm. He had never wanted that; at no time in his life had he wanted that. The only person King ever had considered killing was himself.

* 7 *

King had actually dozed off, and awoke only when the car stopped. "We're here," Rae Borchard said.

A doorman appeared by the car; he took King's suitcase and led them inside what looked like a fortified urban castle. Through a narrow entranceway watched by a stationary TV camera they moved into a foyer half as large as the entire first apartment King had been staying in. The floors were marble. A few chairs and a loveseat were placed against the walls, which boasted a selection of original paintings. Fresh flowers were on the three or four small tables. Obviously this was the place where Dennis Cox had thought they'd be staying.

Dominating the foyer was a semicircular counter, also of marble, that discreetly hid the banks of monitors that were the heart of the building's security system. Two men were on duty; Rae Borchard didn't so much introduce King as she did identify him for them. One of the men took two Polaroid shots of him.

"I don't look like this all the time," King told them, self-consciously fingering his bandage.

The doorman had summoned an elevator for them. He put King's suitcase in the car, murmured something inaudible, and disappeared. The elevator was an ornate affair that had a padded bench to sit on and a painting on one wall to look at. Everything about this building was ornate and luxurious; it went without saying that there'd be no unmanageably heavy windows or itty-bitty TV sets here. *God damn Warren Osterman!* King thought in a rush of fury. *If he'd put us here in the first place, Dennis and Gregory would still be alive!*

Rae Borchard must have read his mind. "This apartment has only three bedrooms," she said. "Warren thought it'd be better if you were all staying at the same place."

The anger went out of King as quickly as it had come. It wasn't Warren Osterman's fault Dennis and Gregory were dead.

The elevator stopped at the twenty-second floor. "It's 2206," Rae said and led the way.

Mimi Hargrove met them at the door. She took one look at King's battered face and burst into tears. "Oh, King!" she cried—and threw both arms around him.

King was so surprised that he dropped his suitcase, barely missing Rae's foot. He put his arms around Mimi and reassured her that he was all right. It wasn't an entirely comfortable clinch, since the top of her head barely reached his chest; they soon broke away. "I look worse than I feel," King said, not entirely truthfully.

"Come inside—shut the door," Mimi answered with an uncharacteristic display of nervousness.

"You're both safe here," Rae said as she and King went in. "You don't have to worry as long as you both stay inside. I'll just put these in the office." She was referring to the armload of King's papers that she carried.

Alone with Mimi, King was aware all over again that she too had lost a partner. "I'm sorry, Mimi. I know you were close to Gregory. How long were you together?"

"Over five years," she sniffed. "He was a friend before he was ever a partner. It was Gregory's idea to start SmartSoft, you know. He brought me in."

King floundered for something comforting to say, and ended up saying the worst thing possible: "Well, you still have three more partners."

"For god's sake, Sauerkraut!" Mimi flared. "We're not talking about replacing a wrecked car, we're talking about a human being! What a *callous* thing to say!"

King thought that over, as calmly as he was able. "You're right, Mimi. It came out callous, but I didn't mean it that way. I was just trying to make you feel better. I'm so doped up on medication that I'm not thinking straight. Please forgive me."

Her hand went to her mouth. "Oh, of course—I should have known. I'm not thinking straight either, and I'm not doped up on anything. I'm sorry I snapped at you, King."

Mimi's apology lifted King's spirits a little. He'd talked himself out of an awkward spot; that didn't happen often. "It doesn't matter," he said magnanimously.

"We've got to relate to each other now," Mimi said earnestly. "We're the only ones left."

Relate what to each other? King wondered. *Ghost stories? Dirty limericks?* He was saved from having to answer by Rae Borchard's return. "I'll show you your room," she said.

He picked up his suitcase and followed, looking over this new apartment that would be home for the next couple of weeks. The place was almost belligerently modern, full of reflecting surfaces and sharp angles. It was all silvers and blacks and grays and whites; the only bright color was provided by the people in it. King liked it.

His bedroom was huge. Double bureau, a wall-mounted mirror that ran from floor to ceiling, two bookshelves, three chairs, a separate dressing room that led to a bathroom. A thick black carpet that seemed to proclaim *Take your shoes off, enjoy!* Cable television, with a thirty-inch screen this time. In one corner a computer work station had been set up. But best of all, to King's eye, was the room-dominating presence of— aha!—a *King*-sized bed. He had to sleep on the diagonal of most beds; he was fully comfortable only in his own king-sized bed at home. And now this one. "Oh yes," King murmured before Rae could ask him if everything was all right.

"Is there anything you need?" she asked instead.

He shook his head, and aggravated the pain that had been thumping dully beneath the surface. "I'm going to take a pill and lie down."

"I'll get you some water." She headed off toward the bathroom.

King flushed with pleasure. Attractive, efficient women didn't usually fetch and carry for him. He fumbled a pain pill out of the vial and took the glass of water Rae brought him.

He felt the effects of the medication almost immediately. Rae was talking about tomorrow's plans, and she said something about Warren Osterman that King didn't get; his head was growing woozier by the second. He flapped a hand vaguely in her direction. "I'm sorry, Rae."

She understood. "I'll leave you alone. Get some sleep."

He didn't hear her leave. He pulled off as much of his clothing as he could manage before collapsing on to the big, long, wide, comfortable bed.

Mimi ordered them something to eat. When she'd seen King stumble out of his bedroom after a three-hour nap, she'd said: "There's lots of stuff in the fridge, but I don't feel like fixing anything and I'm sure you don't either. Is Chinese all right? Or would you rather have an omelet?"

"Chinese is fine."

"I don't know how easy that is to digest—how's your stomach?"

King placed one hand over his midsection. "It seems to be okay," he said, thinking of all the food he'd consumed the day before—and suddenly realized his hand was pressing against bare skin. He glanced down and saw he was wearing nothing but shorts and one black sock. "I'm standing here talking to you in my underwear," he said.

The corner of Mimi's mouth twitched. "Does that embarrass you?"

He thought about it. "No."

"Good. It doesn't bother me, so don't worry about it."

When their food was delivered, they didn't talk much at first; they were both hungry. The spicy Szechuan meal hit the spot, and King got a little boy's kick out of sitting in the formal dining room in his underwear and eating food out of paper cartons. He and Mimi both relaxed once their hunger was blunted. The double tragedy of Dennis Cox's and Gregory Dillard's deaths was having the effect of drawing the two survivors closer together, a not unusual circumstance. King was enjoying the casual, noncompetitive atmosphere that was developing between the two of them. And he rather liked the idea of playing house with Mimi Hargrove.

Unfortunately, she wanted to talk about her husband. "I called him in Vienna," she said. "I caught him right before he left for the Indian Ocean. He wanted to come back."

"Understandable."

"But I wouldn't let him. His work is important too. It's just that Michael is *so* committed to our marriage that sometimes he loses his sense of proportion."

"Did you tell him the police think you might be in danger?"

"Oh, no! Then he *would* come back. But what could he do that the police can't do better? Besides, I don't want him to worry. Michael doesn't always handle stress as well as he should—he's very sensitive, you know. And he does tend to be overprotective."

King made a noncommittal noise. So Mimi was the strong one in the marriage—was that the message he was supposed to get? Obviously she wasn't above paying herself compliments when the opportunity arose. King felt a perverse urge to take

Michael's side. "How would you feel if he kept something like that from you?"

She was silent a moment. "I should hate it," she finally replied. "Because it would imply that he didn't think I was strong enough to handle it . . . is that what you're getting at? Don't misunderstand, King—Michael is strong, very strong, in most circumstances. There are just a few areas where his defense systems aren't quite a hundred percent. I'm one of those areas. I don't know what he'd do if anything happened to me. But that's what you have to expect, I suppose, when you have a marriage in which both partners are as committed as Michael and I are."

King thought of Dennis Cox's hand in her lap and said nothing. Letting yourself get felt up during a business conference evidently didn't count.

"I've thought about going back to California," she went on. "but I think we're both safer here, where the police already know what's going on."

"I've thought of going home too," King lied. "But after seeing this fortress we're staying in . . ."

"Yes, it does make you feel safe, doesn't it?"

King felt a twinge of conscience. This woman was in fear of her life, and all because of him. He longed to tell her she was safe, that no conglomerate of competitors was out to *bump them off*. He got no pleasure from worrying her. "You know, Mimi, maybe everything has been just a series of accidents after all. Even my mugging."

She shook her head. "No."

"The police don't *know* what happened. They're only guessing."

"No, King. Three of us are attacked the same day, and it would have been four if I'd stayed in the apartment Wednesday night. Let's not kid ourselves. Somebody wants us dead—all of us."

King shrugged and let it go.

Mimi told him she'd been the one to walk unsuspecting into the other apartment and discover what had happened there. "You were lucky, King—you didn't have to see that ugly sight. Gregory's body on the floor under the window, blood all over the place and his head missing. I thought I was going to pass out. I barely made it to my bathroom to throw up." She'd used the phone in her room to call the police, and then had stayed there until the police arrived. She'd had to pass through the living room to let them in; she told King she'd kept her eyes on her feet so as not to have to look at what was left of Gregory.

There'd been two uniformed officers at the door, a young one and a not-so-young one. The young one had had the same reaction as Mimi's; he'd taken one look at the headless body and started gagging. Mimi had quickly directed him not to her bathroom but to the nearest one, the one at the end of the hall. The unfortunate young officer had stumbled into the bathroom—and found another dead man in the tub.

"All that time," Mimi said wide-eyed, "all that time I was waiting for the police to get there—I just sat there, totally unaware that there was another corpse in the apartment."

King winced at her way of referring to Dennis. "Mimi, you don't know how much I wish you could have been spared that." He meant it.

"I wish I could have too. *You* certainly were no help. Getting yourself mugged at a time like that—and in Central Park, too! Couldn't you have picked something more original?" Only half joking. "What hospital did they take you to?"

King blinked. "I don't know. I didn't ask."

"You didn't *ask?*"

"It just never occurred to me."

Anyone else would have laughed at his absentmindedness, but not Mimi. "It never occurred to you. You know,

Sauerkraut, sometimes I can't believe you're real."

"Don't call me that."

She made a hand gesture that could have meant anything. The tension lasted only a minute, though; they cleared away the remains of their meal and by mutual unspoken agreement headed toward the apartment's office, which was a great deal larger than the office in the other apartment.

They spent the next few hours going over the weapons platform specifications—asking each other questions, getting organized, trying to spot potential trouble areas. They lost themselves in the work until they reached what looked like a reasonable stopping point; at twelve o'clock King took another pain pill and told Mimi good night.

It was only after he'd showered and crawled back into the big bed that a possible explanation occurred to him as to why Mimi was so adamant about their being in danger . . . a rather warped explanation that he didn't care for at all. *Maybe she likes being thought important enough to kill.* King shuddered; the idea was uncharitable even for him, and he resolutely put it out of his mind.

The following morning an army of strangers descended upon them. For an hour and a half the army dusted, vacuumed, cleaned up the kitchen, scoured out the bathrooms, changed the bed linen and towels, emptied the wastebaskets, smiled incessantly, and refused to accept money. Then, in an eyeblink, they were gone.

"Do you know," King said wonderingly, "that is the first time in my life I've ever known anyone in New York to turn down money when it was offered."

Mimi considered his remark literally, as she did everything. "It's probably in their contract that they can't accept tips from guests," she said. "Don't worry, I'm sure the fee MechoTech pays them is outrageous."

While the army was in the midst of waging its war on dirt, Rae Borchard's secretary had stopped by with a new watch and briefcase for King. The watch was beautiful, and far more expensive than what King would have bought for himself. Not a Rolex; that would have been too obvious. Dennis Cox would have admired it, though; he'd owned at least a dozen watches, all of them of status-symbol level of expensiveness.

King remembered something he should have taken care of the day before. He went to his room and put in a call to Gale Fredericks in Pittsburgh. Normally she didn't make a practice of going in to the lab on Saturdays, but under the present circumstances . . .

She was there. "Oh, King—I tried to reach you all day yesterday! Are you all right?"

"Well, yes, I guess so. I was mugged."

She gave a little cry and ordered him to return to Pittsburgh immediately.

It took some doing, but he managed to convince her that his mugging had no connection with Dennis's accident—he stressed the word *accident*. They exchanged expressions of anguish over Dennis's death, heartfelt on both sides. Gale had learned what had happened from a local news reporter who'd shown up at Keystone Robotics seeking "reactions" from those who knew him. Gale had not been especially fond of Dennis, but she was shocked by both the suddenness of his death and the means of it. Now she was clearly more worried about what King was going through, a misplaced concern he did nothing to dispel.

Gale had never met Gregory Dillard, but his death both disturbed and frightened her. "Two fatal accidents at the same time? Doesn't that strike you as odd?" she asked.

"It strikes me as very odd. But that's what happened, Gale." He asked her to look in Dennis's office for the list of credit card numbers and notify the appropriate people that King's cards had been stolen.

She said she'd take care of it. "Oh, I almost forgot. A woman named Shawna Wallace called here asking for a King Sarsowitch—that's the way she pronounced it. She said you'd given her your card but you forgot to tell her your New York phone number."

King had to think a moment before he remembered who she was. Ah, yes—Shawna of the elegant height and the vampire-bite tattoo. So her last name was Wallace, and she wanted his New York phone number. "Did you give it to her?"

"No, but I took down hers in case you wanted to call her back. Got a pencil?"

"Yes," he lied. "Go ahead." King barely listened as Gale read off the number. He'd liked Shawna, but he had no intention of calling her. Because Shawna could tell anyone who was interested, such as the police, that one King Sarcowicz was healthy and unmugged at a time he was supposed to be lying helpless in Central Park.

"Want to read that back?" Gale asked.

"No, I got it. But speaking of phone numbers, do *you* have a pencil?" He told her his new number and the address of the building where he was now staying. "Gale, try not to worry. We'll come through this, you'll see. Just hold the fort until I get back."

She said she would and they both hung up. King still had his hand on the receiver when the phone rang. It was Rae Borchard, saying she'd set up a dental appointment for King and a limousine would pick him up and wait to bring him back. She made it quite clear that he was not to go wandering about the streets.

King meekly followed instructions. It was so unncessary, all these precautions, but he could hardly say so. He kept the appointment; the dentist inserted an appliance to hold his two wobbly teeth immobile until the damaged bone that held them had time to regenerate. King returned to the apartment to find Warren Osterman waiting for him, sitting regally in the middle of one of the living room's two white sofas. Mimi was out on a balcony that opened off the living room, enjoying the sun.

"Howya feeling, King?" the older man wanted to know. "Up to tackling a problem? You look like hell."

The bruise on King's face had turned a bilious greenish-yellow overnight. That morning he'd taken off the gauze bandage, which was starting to get dirty, and replaced it with a couple of Band-Aids. "I'm feeling a lot better today," he said truthfully. "My head's stopped hurting—that was the worst thing. What's the problem that needs tackling?"

"The Defense Department. I sold the four of you as a team, and now they're wondering who's going to take Dennis's and Gregory's places. Wait a minute," he said as King started to protest, "I know you think you and Mimi can handle it, and maybe you can. But we don't have the final say. It's weird, but these two murders convinced the boys in Defense that your team had to have something special going for it if a competitor's out to get you. But they want the team back at full strength."

"Easier said than done."

"I know. How do you replace Dennis Cox?" Osterman took a deep breath. "Believe it or not, I'd come to like Dennis. Gregory Dillard I could take or leave alone, but Dennis I liked. And I think he was coming around to my way of thinking—about the merger, I mean."

King frowned, not following. "What merger is that?"

Osterman stared at him. "The merger of MechoTech and Keystone, of course," he said patiently.

King stared back. "I never heard anything about any merger."

The two men realized the truth at the same time. Osterman laughed. "That sly son of a bitch—he never told you, did he? Ha! I had no idea. Well, to put it simply, I want Keystone to be part of the MechoTech family, and I think Dennis did too. He was playing the game, holding out for the best terms he could get."

"And when you two reached agreement, he'd present it to me as a *fait accompli*, is that it?"

"I suppose so. You usually followed his recommendations on financial matters, didn't you?"

"Yeah. That's what I did." *Dammit.* King was thunderstruck. A merger with MechoTech? Dennis had known King wouldn't go for it; that's why he'd put off telling him. "Warren, I can't deal with this now."

"I don't expect you to. I'll send another copy of the proposal around in a few weeks—we'll talk about it then. You know, Dennis must have been planning to tell you this weekend. He couldn't count on my not mentioning the merger to you. It would all have been straightened out in a few days."

Never speak ill of the dead? King walked over to the glass doors that opened on to the balcony and looked out at Mimi. She'd taken some papers and a legal pad out with her, but now she just lay back in her chair with her eyes closed. Dennis Cox wouldn't have minded seeing their company's individuality swallowed up by the MechoTech giant if it meant a chance for him to get ahead. Perhaps he saw himself as Warren Osterman's eventual successor? His partner had never cared shit about Keystone; all he'd cared about was Dennis Cox.

"King, you've got to get a replacement," Warren Osterman was saying from behind him. "Not only for the project but for your company as well. You need a money man, a manager. Mimi's in pretty good shape—she's got three other partners she can draw on. But you . . . ?"

"I know, I know."

"Don't wait too long, King." Something in Osterman's tone made King look a question at him. "The first time I talked to Mimi after Dennis and Gregory were killed," the older man said, "she was quick to point out that all the work Dennis would have done on the project was now going to fall on your shoulders. And she made no bones about saying you couldn't handle it. She wants me to make her project leader."

Jesus. Stab-in-the-back time. But King had to admire her chutzpah, even while resenting it. "She doesn't miss a bet, does she? What did you tell her?"

"I told her her request was premature. King, I want *you* running this project, not Mimi or any other software designer. But she has a point. You need somebody like Dennis to take care of the organizational details for you."

King went back and sat down on the sofa beside him. "I may have someone."

Osterman's eyebrows went up. "That's great. Who—"

"Not yet. I'm going to have to do some fast talking and it may take a few days. But I'm not going to try to run the project by myself, I promise you. Let me talk to my first choice, and if that doesn't work out . . . well, then I'll get somebody else."

A faint smile appeared on Osterman's face. "You seem very sure of yourself."

"It's a solvable problem, Warren. We're not going to lose the contract, take my word for it."

Osterman studied him a minute and then said, "All right! You get a replacement for Dennis, Mimi calls in one of her other partners, and we proceed as planned. In the meantime, the two of you stay put. We don't want 'em getting another shot at you."

King laughed shortly, irritated anew by all the unnecessary precautions. "Warren, this morning a whole platoon of cleaning people invaded this apartment. Couldn't the guy with the vacuum cleaner or the lady with the Glass-Plus have been paid to do a little extra job? Do you know for a fact that *none* of those people can be gotten to? And they're not the only ones who were here. Rae Borchard's secretary stopped by . . .

and don't forget the limo driver who took me to get my teeth fixed—what about him? Then I walk into the office of a dentist I never heard of before and I'm surrounded by a fleet of assistants, not to mention a couple of other patients waiting their turn. That's over twenty people who could have had 'another shot' at me today if they'd wanted to."

Osterman was suddenly looking his age. "My god."

"And what about Mimi, right now?" King pressed on. "Out there on that balcony, exposed like that? Somebody with a high-powered rifle in another building could pick her off easy as pie. We can't guard against everything, Warren. There's just no point trying."

The other man rubbed his forehead with a clenched fist. "I must be slowing down. I didn't think of any of that." He levered himself up off the sofa with difficulty, like an old man. He went to the balcony and told Mimi to come inside. As soon as she understood why, she hurried back in, looking frightened and stammering out a thank-you. "Thank King," Osterman said. "He thought of it."

She threw King a surprised but grateful look and sank down in a chair some distance from the balcony doors. King had meant to use Mimi as an example of how impossible it was to be on guard all the time; but if the other two chose to interpret it as concern for Mimi's safety, he wasn't going to argue. Osterman said he'd be in touch later and left.

The minute he was gone, King called Gale Fredericks and told her to catch the next plane to New York.

King and Mimi were hard at work making out a list of design priorities when Sergeant Ivan Malecki paid them a visit. King was annoyed; he didn't like being interrupted when the work was going well, and he didn't like the way Malecki so obviously appreciated Mimi's good looks. There were a time and a place for everything; he expected the police to be more professional. "Anything new, Sergeant?" he asked testily.

Sergeant Malecki reluctantly dragged his attention from Mimi to concentrate on the matter at hand. "I brought some pictures for you to look at," he said, plopping a thick mailing envelope down on a table in the office. "See if any of the guys who attacked you are in there."

King remembered. "Oh, that's right—Officer, uh, Jones wanted me to look at mug shots. I forgot all about it. Sergeant Malecki, the guys who attacked me were just roughneck kids. They didn't have anything to do with what happened to Dennis and Gregory."

"Some of the kids we got files on would kill their grandmothers for a twenty-dollar bill. I couldn't bring all the pictures we got, but those are the ones we think most likely. Take a look."

King opened the envelope and about forty photos spilled out, four-by-five glossies. He stacked them up neatly and started looking. Sergeant Malecki took advantage of the time to carry on a low-tone conversation with Mimi.

Right away King spotted the leader of the gang of teen-aged muggers who'd got him. He could even hear the young hoodlum's voice in his head as he stared at the kid's image. He quickly tossed the picture aside with the other rejects. Toward the end of the stack he found one that he felt fairly sure was another member of the gang. He finished the rest and said, "I'm sorry, Sergeant. It wasn't any of these kids."

"You sure? You did that awfully fast. Take another look."

"A lot of these kids are black or Hispanic. I told Officer Jones the muggers were white."

"Yeah, well, there's always a chance you're not remembering right. Look at the pictures again. Take your time."

So King went through the motions of looking at them all again, studying each photo carefully . . . and obviously. This time when he said no, Sergeant Malecki took his word for it.

"Thass too bad," the sergeant said. "My partner and I were sure at least one of 'em would be in there."

King barely remembered Malecki's partner. "Uh, Sergeant Lurch?"

"Larch. Tell me something. This project you're both working on—who's paying for it?"

Mimi answered him. "Well, DARPA funds the initial research, but once the Army approves the working model—"

"Hold it. DARPA?"

"Defense Advanced Research Projects Agency," Mimi explained. "It's a branch of the Defense Department that searches for new weapons technology. They fund research on everything from talking computers to exploding postage stamps—anything that might provide an edge in the arms race. Our job here is to put together a practical electromagnetic gun platform for field combat."

"Lotta bucks involved?"

"A lot."

Sergeant Malecki nodded. "Who would get the project if you two pulled out?"

Mimi shook her head. "There's no waiting list, Sergeant. DARPA would have to start all over, from scratch."

The sergeant gathered up the pictures and put them back in the envelope. "Well, somebody thinks they've got a crack at it. Mr. Sarcowicz, you told my partner you left the apartment Thursday around nine or ten. It had to be closer to nine. The way we figure it, you must have walked out only minutes before the killer got there. Did you see anybody? In the hallway, on the elevator?"

"I didn't see anyone at all," King said. "The hall and the elevator were both empty." He'd run down the stairs instead of using the elevator, as a matter of fact, but he didn't want to have to think up a credible reason for that. "How can you be sure I left at nine instead of ten?"

"Time of death. Gregory Dillard died at nine-seventeen, so you had to be gone a little while before that."

King swallowed. "Nine-seventeen. Ah, I didn't know the medical examiner could pinpoint time of death so precisely."

"He can't. We're going by other evidence. Y'know, somebody's head comes falling down out of the sky, people notice."

Mimi made a sound of distress. "Sorry. But we got eight witnesses saw Dillard's head hit, and two of 'em are friends who were checking their watches when it happened. Nine-seventeen, on the button."

King didn't like where this was going. "I still have trouble believing it was anything other than an accident."

"Oh, it was no accident. No chance of that. Because there was somebody else in the apartment at the time."

Mimi gasped. "How do you know that?"

"The witnesses say there was a man standing at the window. They couldn't make out the feaures, he was too high up. It couldn't have been Dennis Cox, because Mr. Sarcowicz here told my partner Cox was already soaking in the tub when he left. That means there was another man in the apartment Thursday morning."

King felt as if he were drowning. "How do your witnesses know which apartment the man was in?"

"One of 'em had enough presence of mind to count the floors. It was that apartment, all right. Gregory Dillard must have let this other man in, and he must have trusted him to hold the window while he leaned out to feed his one-footed pigeon. He was someone Dillard knew."

"Wait a minute," King said in a strangled voice, "then it *could* have been an accident! Gregory let a friend in, the friend held the window, the window slipped and killed Gregory, and the friend got spooked and ran! Couldn't it have happened that way?"

Sergeant Malecki got up to leave. "Then how do you explain Dennis Cox?"

Dennis. King had no answer.

"Look, I don't want to alarm you two any more than I have to," the sergeant said, "but if the killer was someone Gregory Dillard knew, then he's probably someone *you* know too. I'd be real careful about who I let in here, if I was you."

"Count on it," Mimi said grimly.

"Lock the door after me," Malecki said, and left.

Mimi locked up while King stared unseeing at the door that had just closed, his carefully rebuilt sense of safety crumbling all about him.

* 8 *

King told Mimi he needed to take a pain pill and lie down for a bit. It was true; everything in his body had started hurting. In his room with the door closed, he stood in the middle of the floor and shook. Good god—how easily he'd allowed himself to be lulled into a false sense of safety! Going about his work on the project with Mimi, as if all that unpleasantness were over and done with!

All along he'd been hoping the police would not be able to pinpoint the time of death so exactly; with the time of his mugging moved up to late morning, he needed a medical pronouncement of the vaguer sort—*Death occurred between nine and eleven A.M.*, that sort of thing. He'd completely forgotten about Gregory's head tumbling down to the street, an event unusual enough to attract attention even in New York.

How could anyone in his right mind overlook a thing like that? *Maybe that's the problem,* King thought; *maybe I'm not in my right mind.* He swallowed a pill dry and stretched out on the big bed. Eight people, Sergeant Malecki had said, eight people had seen him standing at the window after he'd unintentionally decapitated Gregory Dillard. The shock had momentarily paralyzed him; he'd just stood there and let the witnesses on the street below get a look at him.

Unintentionally decapitated. How in the hell did you explain that you'd *unintentionally decapitated* someone?

How long would the police keep looking for a killer among MechoTech's competitors? How long before they gave it up as hopeless and moved the case to the unsolved murders file? Or, more likely, *how long before they started suspecting King Sarcowicz?*

King tried to think. Would the police have any specific reason to suspect him? He had no cause for wanting either Dennis or Gregory dead. He was not better off with them dead—in fact, he was worse off. Dennis was no friend, but King needed him. Warren Osterman understood that. Mimi Hargrove understood that. But would Sergeants Malecki and Larch understand?

King sat up in the bed. The conclusion was obvious: he'd have to find a way to make them understand—subtly, without seeming to. He'd have to convince them that the success of the project had depended as much on Dennis Cox as it did on King Sarcowicz; that would be a bitter pill, but he'd swallow it. Persuading the police . . . it could be managed. He would have to manage it.

Something nagged at him: if he could overlook an event so gruesomely obvious as Gregory's head smashing into the sidewalk, what else might he have missed? Let's see, he'd spoken to a lot of strangers on Thursday, during his flight from the apartment . . . starting with that guy among the garbage trucks on Pier 97. Then he'd gone into that first restaurant, ordered pastrami, tried to start a conversation with the kid with the green Mohawk, paid his bill, and left.

Whoa. He'd left a tip in cash, but to pay the bill he'd used *a credit card.* With a new sense of horror King realized he'd left a credit trail all the way across Fifty-seventh Street. He jumped off the bed and looked for his billfold a moment or two before remembering it had been stolen. He'd wanted to destroy his receipts, but his adolescent muggers had probably just thrown them away; they'd have no reason to keep them. Not for the first time King thought that the mugging was the luckiest thing that could have happened to him, god bless those vicious little bastards.

Also not for the first time, King wished he weren't so tall and therefore so noticeable. If those two police detectives started looking on Fifty-seventh Street, they were bound to find someone who remembered him. The waiter in the Russian Tea Room who'd cleaned up his spilled wine. The machine-hating old man in the Sutton Place park, whatever it was called. The kid Ricky, who thought his newly widowed mom was dallying with the family lawyer; King had told him his name. And Shawna—he'd actually given Shawna one of his business cards. He'd left tracks everywhere he'd been.

Don't panic—think. All right. How would the police know to check Fifty-seventh Street in the first place? They had no reason to pick one street out of the hundreds in Manhattan and go knocking on every door. And Fifty-seventh was such a big street, people coming and going all the time. The chances of the police's finding any of the folks he'd talked to were really pretty slim, perhaps nonexistent. As King thought about it, he slowly became convinced that he had little to fear from Fifty-seventh Street.

All the same, he'd make a point of avoiding that particular thoroughfare for the rest of his natural life. He'd have to remember to feign ignorance if someone asked him where Carnegie Hall was. Or the Hard Rock Café. If anyone mentioned Pier 97, he'd ask what kind of ships docked there. All he had to do was keep his wits about him and he'd be safe. Stay frosty, don't get rattled.

A light tap sounded at his bedroom door. "King, are you awake?"

"I'm awake, Mimi. Come on in."

She looked troubled. After an awkward pause, Mimi blurted out: "I think I know who killed Gregory and Dennis!"

King's knees buckled and he sat down on the side of the bed, hard. *So much for staying frosty.* "Who?" he croaked.

Mimi took a deep breath and said, "Rae Borchard."

King was so surprised he forgot to feel relieved. "Rae Borchard? Why on earth would Rae Borchard want to kill Dennis and Gregory?"

She found a chair and sat down before answering. "I can only guess about the motive—but the thing is, the killer was somebody Gregory knew. He let him or her into the apartment."

"That's what the police think. So?"

"So, how many people could that be? That he'd let in, I mean. It just doesn't make sense to think that Gregory had called a friend and arranged to meet him at nine in the morning of a workday. I'm not sure he even had any friends in New York. King, who would be *likely* to come to the apartment? There are only two—Warren Osterman and Rae Borchard."

"Well . . ."

"You know it's not Warren. Why would he call us all here and try to kill us? Besides, Warren's an old man. He's not all that strong. He might have been able to surprise Gregory at the window, but surely Dennis could have stopped him from tossing that little TV set into the tub." She crossed her legs, uncrossed them, crossed them the other way; nervous. "So that leaves Rae Borchard."

King tried to visualize the scene that had never taken place, Rae Borchard walking into the bathroom and picking up a TV set she had no way of knowing was in there . . . ah. He pointed that out to Mimi.

"She could have improvised," Mimi said. "Maybe she had a gun in her purse, but when she got there she found she didn't have to use it."

Uh-huh. "But why would Dennis have been able to stop Warren from throwing the TV into the water but not Rae?"

"Well, think of the scene. Dennis is lying in the tub, stark naked, when this attractive woman walks in and looks at him. Dennis would have loved that. You know he would. He wouldn't have paid any attention if she started fiddling with the television."

Reasonable, King thought. *Utterly wrong, but reasonable.* "Okay, but what's her motive?"

Mimi took a moment to get her thoughts in order. She said, "This is only a guess, but I think it's right. You know Rae is Warren's heir apparent."

"I'd wondered about that. Go on."

"He's been training her to take over MechoTech when he retires, but nothing is carved in stone. She could still lose it. I think Rae Borchard saw Gregory and me as potential rivals. It was Gregory and *me* she was after—Dennis was killed because he just happened to be in the apartment."

King scrunched up his eyes. "I don't follow that. Why—"

"King, I'm going to tell you something in confidence. Will you give me your word not to repeat it?"

"Yes, of course. What is it?"

"Warren Osterman has proposed a merger of MechoTech and SmartSoft. That would have put both Gregory and me in the running as Warren's possible successor."

King felt his mouth drop open. "Why, that wily old fox! He's after Keystone too—I just found out about that myself."

Then it was Mimi's mouth that dropped open. "He wants both our companies? That means you and Dennis . . . oh my. Then she'd meant to kill Dennis all along, and now you and I are still in her way—"

"Hold it, Mimi. It's a nice theory, but you're wrong. It couldn't have been Rae Borchard."

"Why not?"

"Well . . . remember the witnesses on the street? They said it was a man they saw standing at the window."

"Rae has short hair. If she was wearing a tie and jacket, nobody would have been able to tell the difference from that distance."

King just looked at her.

"Well, it's possible!" Mimi said crossly. "All right, Mr. Know-it-all, who do you think killed them?"

"I think," King said firmly, "I think both deaths were accidents."

"And the man the witnesses saw at the window?"

King shrugged. "Maybe there was no man. Or maybe the one witness counted the floors wrong and our mystery man was in a different apartment. The witnesses had just had a nasty shock, remember, and they couldn't have been thinking too clearly. They might be mistaken about what they thought they saw."

Mimi made a sound of contempt. "Two separate fatal accidents—same time, same place. You're going to stick to that lamebrained theory?"

"Like glue," said King.

Gale Fredericks had taken King at his word when he said catch the next plane to New York. She showed up at the apartment that evening with a nylon carry-all slung over her shoulder and wearing a Saturday work outfit of jeans, sneakers, and sweater. Mimi, of course, was the essence of California chic—designer clothing, full make-up, earrings and bracelets (no gold chains). Suprisingly, neither woman seemed to find anything unusual in the way the other was dressed.

King made the introductions; Gale murmured something to Mimi but couldn't take her eyes off King's bruised face. "King, you look terrible."

"You should have seen him yesterday," Mimi said wryly.
"A lovely royal purple."
"Was anything inside broken?"
"Some bone that holds a couple of teeth in place," King said, "but it's being taken care of. I'm all right, Gale, really." She pulled her eyes away from his bruises and fished an envelope out of her purse. "I brought you some cash. And I called the agency your credit cards are registered with—they'll notify everybody and get new cards issued."
"Oh, bless you. You're a lifesaver. Come on, I'll show you your room."
He took her to the apartment's one remaining bedroom, explaining something of the layout on the way. "There are only the three bedrooms, but there's also an office, a games room, and what Mimi calls a media room. A place to watch big-screen TV."
Gale glanced around her room, impressed. "This is some place, isn't it? I could learn to live like this."
King grinned. "Me too."
"The guards downstairs made me prove I'm really Gale Fredericks before they'd let me in. Then they wouldn't let me come up until they'd taken two pictures of me."
"Yes, they're very security-conscious here." King was childishly proud of himself for having remembered to notify the guards that Gale was coming; that was the sort of thing he'd always left to Dennis.
Gale took a deep breath and said what was on her mind. "King, you're in danger, aren't you? It's not over. Whoever killed Dennis is still after you."
He shook his head. "Nobody is after me. That's just the way the police think. They *assume* that two accidents couldn't take place at the same time. But it can happen—and it did."
"But you're just making assumptions, too! You don't know they were both accidents. How can you take such

a risk with your own life?"

"There's no risk, I tell you! What would be the point in killing off the entire design team? We're all replaceable." Then it hit him. "You think I'm putting you in danger too? Just by bringing you here? Oh, Gale, I could never do that! Do you really think I'd ask you to come if there were any risk?"

She didn't answer, but turned away from him uneasily. *That's exactly what she does think,* King thought, stunned—and grudgingly acknowledged she had reason. It was precisely the sort of careless thing he'd been doing all his life; of course she'd think he'd just blunder on, giving no thought to the trouble he might be causing other people. King had to admit she was justified; it was probably the way everyone saw him.

He made an effort to salvage the situation. "Gale, do you know any of the details of what happened?" He went on to explain about the window in the other apartment, about how heavy it was and how it wouldn't stay up without someone holding it. He told her about the time he and Mimi together had had to struggle to keep it from slipping. "Gregory should never have tried to hold it up by himself. But Dennis was in the tub and I was already gone, and I guess he wanted to put some bread out before the pigeon flew away. He should have waited." King was pleased with how reasonable that sounded. "The police weren't there, they don't know how it was."

Gale was nodding. "It certainly sounds like an accident, the way you tell it. But Dennis—at the same time?"

King told her the same lie he'd told Sergeant Larch. "It's truly ironic—I'd warned him about that very thing. I saw him going into the bathroom carrying the television and I said be sure not to plug it in near the tub. He just said *yeah, yeah,* kind of annoyed, and went on in." King gave a mirthless laugh. "Electrocuting himself—that's the sort of thing *I'd* do, not Dennis. Not Dennis." He tried to look properly bemused.

Gale was all but convinced. "What does Warren Osterman think?"

King took her hand and led her to a settee beneath a window. "He agrees with the police." How was that for being upfront with her? "Warren has aged a lot since the last time I saw him," not quite so upfront. "This is his last big project and he's scared to death something will happen to screw it up. He's seeing boogeymen in every shadow. He's even had security checks run on the people who clean this apartment, for crying out loud." Wherever had this new-found talent for lying come from? "Warren is nervous for another reason as well."

"What's that?"

"He's supervising the project, but the real running of it is going to be in the hands of his assistant and apparent successor in the business. A woman named Rae Borchard. She seems quite competent, but Warren's bound to worry."

Gale was silent for a long time. Finally she sighed and said, "Then Dennis's death really was an accident?"

"It really was. Believe me."

"Poor Dennis. What an awful way to die. We were never close friends . . . but still, Keystone won't be the same without him there. I counted on him, to take care of things—you know?"

"I know. I counted on him too."

"He will be missed." She stood up briskly, deliberately breaking her gloomy mood. "Have you had time to to think what you're going to do? Run Keystone by yourself, look for a new partner? You know, hiring a manager might be a good move . . . if you could find someone with a robotics background."

"That's a possibility. Do you know anybody?"

"Not offhand. Let me think about it." Then Gale announced that she had to have a shower before one more minute passed; the air-conditioning on the plane hadn't been working too well and she felt hot and sticky. King told her he'd be in the office and left her to herself.

Mimi was already in the office. She looked up from her work and asked, "Is Gale going to take Dennis's place?"

"If I can talk her into it."

"Talk her into it? She has to be talked into it?"

"Well, Gale has this thing about weapons and the military. She hates them."

Mimi rolled her eyes. "Still living in the sixties, is she? Don't you have anyone more motivated?"

"I'm sure I do, but Gale's the best designer."

"Then just *assign* her to the project, King. She does work for you, doesn't she?"

"She might quit."

Mimi thought about that. "But you want her anyway. Is she that good?"

King nodded. "She's that good. What's more, she can stand working with me for long stretches of time without flipping out. This project needs Gale."

"And you're the one who's going to talk her into it. Well, good luck . . . that wasn't sarcastic, I meant it. It's time we got rolling. I've already decided which of my partners is going to replace Gregory."

"You've decided."

She smiled. "I'm senior partner now. What's Gale doing?"

"Taking a shower. She'll be right in."

Mimi stood up and gathered her papers together. "Then I'd better leave you alone. I wouldn't want to cramp your style."

"Ah, Mimi, you could never do that," King said gallantly. Mimi gave him one of her humorless stares and left.

King had to postpone making his pitch, though. Gale had barely finished her shower, her hair still wet, when Mimi came back to announce that the other of the two detectives assigned to their case had just shown up. The three of them went into the living room, where Marian Larch stood frankly gawking. "All this space . . . and nobody actually lives here," she greeted them incredulously. Then she spotted Gale. "Hello. I'm Detective Sergeant Larch, NYPD."

Gale stuck out a hand. "Sergeant Larch—I'm Gale Fredericks. Keystone Robotics."

The two women shook hands. "Ah ha," said Sergeant Larch. "Just in from Pittsburgh?"

"That's right."

The sergeant looked straight at King. "Dennis Cox's replacement?"

Gale shook her head while King said, "Ah, the question is premature, Sergeant."

The detective got the message; she changed the subject and told them Dennis's parents had just made arrangements to have their son's body shipped back to Pennsylvania for burial.

"Oh, good heavens!" Mimi said, slapping a hand to the side of her face. "I didn't even think of that! I should have done something about Gregory—"

"It's all taken care of," Sergeant Larch reassured her. "Mrs. Dillard made the arrangements yesterday."

"Karen Dillard? She's here?"

"Not now. She flew back to California last night."

"Without getting in touch with me?"

There was an awkward pause. "That is odd, isn't it?" Sergeant Larch said. "Why do you suppose she didn't call you?"

Mimi looked uneasy. "I don't know. I know she's feeling terrible, but you'd think she'd want to get in touch with . . ."

"The survivors?"

Mimi didn't answer. King knew why Dennis's parents hadn't gotten in touch with him; he'd never met them. The sergeant was speaking to King. "Mr. Sarcowicz, I came to ask you not to go to your partner's funeral—his parents have scheduled it for Tuesday. We'd prefer you to stay right here where we can keep an eye on you."

"I understand, Sergeant. Although these precautions aren't really necessary."

"Your opinion, not ours. Will you stay in New York?"

"Yes, yes." Testily.

"Maybe you can have someone go to the funeral in your place."

"I'll go," Gale volunteered. "I'd be going anyway." King smiled his thanks.

"What about Gregory's funeral?" Mimi asked.

"Mrs. Dillard said there wouldn't be any. She had the body cremated, since the head was smashed beyond the possibility of reconstruction. But she told me the last thing she needed right now was to preside over some public lamentation where she'd be required to listen politely to murmured clichés of condolence from people who only wanted to be *seen* grieving her husband's death. I think she's planning a memorial service of some kind in a year's time."

"Well!" Mimi exclaimed. "If that isn't just like Karen!"

"This is a stressful time for her, Mrs. Hargrove," the detective said kindly. "Let her do it her way." Mimi sulked, didn't answer. Sergeant Larch shifted gears again. "What about Mr. Dillard's replacement on your project? Do you have someone?"

"Another one of my partners will be taking his place. He won't be flying in for a couple of weeks, though—not until King and I finish some preliminary work we're doing."

That was news to King. She was shutting her partner out of the initial planning?

"Well, that's all I came here for, to make sure both of you remained in town. And stay indoors!"

"Yes, ma'am," King said, not at all sarcastically.

The minute the police detective was gone, Mimi burst out: "That Karen! Just *ignoring* me, as if I weren't even here!"

Gale tried to play peacemaker. "She had a lot on her mind, Mimi. I'm sure it wasn't deliberate."

"Oh, it was deliberate, all right! For a long time I've suspected she didn't like me . . . she's always been so-o-o polite to me, you know? Like, here is one of Gregory's horrible business associates and I've got to be nice to her for his sake! Now this dreadful thing happens and she—"

King interrupted her. "Why isn't your other partner coming for two weeks?"

"What? Oh, something he's working on won't be finished until then. Don't worry, I'll fill him in on whatever you and I decide."

Neatly excluding Gale, King noticed. Mimi was up to something—another power play of some sort, one she was counting on to put her in charge of the project? King smiled. Earlier, such a possibility would have worried him, even depressed him. But not now; a man who was apparently getting away with causing the deaths of two people wasn't so easily cowed. Now, he was more than willing to take on Mimi Hargrove.

In fact, he was champing at the bit.

Several hours later, King and Gale sat on the dark balcony looking at New York's nightscape. King had opened one of two bottles of champagne he'd found in the refrigerator—not that there was anything to celebrate, but it made a nice touch. Mimi had discreetly stayed out of sight; right then she was in the media room watching a movie.

Gale was disturbed; King could feel the unhappiness flowing out of her from the chair next to his. She was dead set against Keystone's doing military work; it wasn't just a socially-conscious pose on her part. King felt a twinge of conscience about trying to ride roughshod over her convictions, but only a twinge. He'd gotten her to look at the platform specifications and the reports on the earlier design teams' failures; as he'd hoped, she immediately got caught up in the problems the platforms presented, intrigued by the project itself while remaining disapproving of its purpose.

King had wisely kept quiet, letting her read and doodle on a notepad and think about it as much as she wanted. She'd asked some questions; he'd answered them. At last she'd looked up and sighed. "I can see how easy it is to get caught up in something like this," she'd said. "I understand, King, I really do. But please don't ask me to work on it—I just can't."

"But I am asking you," he'd replied. "I'm asking you to work with *me*. The platform is a challenge I can't meet alone. But the two of us together can."

She'd been made uneasy by his putting it on near-personal terms like that, but that was all right. He'd try anything to shake her holier-than-thou attitude. He'd gone on to point out that for every potential weapon someone had ever dreamed up, someone else had found a way to make it work; there would be an electromagnetic gun platform eventually whether Keystone designed it or not. Then he'd argued that any country that didn't take steps to defend itself in these days of high-tech weaponry was simply asking to be attacked. No, he couldn't guarantee the politicians would not use the platform offensively; who could guarantee anything politicians might do? But this gun platform was *needed*, Gale, don't you see that?

He wasn't sure how much of that he believed himself, but at least she was listening. At midnight he'd called a break. He'd poured the champagne and then suggested they go out on the balcony. He'd left the balcony lights off, and the darkness had helped mask the tension a little.

King cleared his throat. "Gale, I have to confess to being a bit underhanded with you. I've held back my trump card until last."

A half moan, half laugh. "I can hardly wait."
Say it; take the plunge. "I want you to replace Dennis in more than just this project. I want you to be my new partner in Keystone Robotics. Half the business will be yours." She was silent; King began to wish he'd turned the balcony lights on so he could see her face. "Gale?"

She finally spoke. "That's some bribe, King."

"It's no bribe. Whether you decide to work on the gun platform with me or not, I still want you as my partner. And I can prove it. If you agree, we'll have new partnership papers drawn up immediately. *Before* you decide about the platform."

The balcony lights suddenly came on; Gale stood by the switch, staring at him. "Are you serious?"

"Do you think I'd joke about a thing like that? Of course I'm serious!"

"But I don't have the kind of money to buy in—"

"You won't need it. My partnership agreement with Dennis states that in the event of the death of one partner, the surviving partner has first option to buy the deceased partner's share. I'm not sure who Dennis's heir is—his parents, or maybe his ex-wife. But whoever it is, that person is legally obligated to sell me Dennis's share of the business if I want to buy it. I will then sell you that share for one dollar."

She inhaled sharply. "So in effect you are *giving* me half of Keystone."

"I consider it an investment. I need you. For one thing, no competitor can hire you away from me if you're my partner."

"And for another," she said wryly, "you're counting on my sense of gratitude to bring me around to working on the gun platform. That plus my new vested interest in the company, of course."

"That's one reason I want you as my partner," King replied, deadpan. "You're so good at reading my mind."

She actually laughed at that. "King, I'm overwhelmed!"

"Don't be overwhelmed. Be a partner. Say yes."

"But Dennis actually *managed* Keystone. I'm a designer—I've never run a company!"

"Gale. Ever since you came to Keystone, you've been doing on a small scale exactly what Dennis did on a larger one. You're the one who keeps me on track, takes care of the paperwork, sees that we meet schedules, orders the supplies, all that sort of thing that I admit I've been careless about in the past. You can do it. Besides, I've decided I've been inexcusably negligent. I'm going to start paying more attention to details of the business from now on."

She just smiled at that.

"But if the paperwork starts to keep you away from designing, then we hire a manager." He grinned. "That'd be one of *your* responsibilities—finding someone." King paused for breath; he'd played his trump card, but Gale hadn't yet followed suit. Time for the ace up his sleeve. "But there's something you should know. Warren Osterman wants a merger between Keystone and MechoTech."

"No!" she cried instinctively.

"No, absolutely. But Dennis was in favor of it. He was negotiating with Warren behind my back."

Gale was speechless.

"So you see why I need a partner I can trust," King went on. "Warren Osterman has a lot of clout in Washington. We're going to have to find a way to say no without alienating him—we still need MechoTech. For a while longer, at any rate. I'm hoping you care enough about Keystone to help me see this through."

She didn't answer. King looked at her standing there hugging herself, her eyes glazed, and decided he'd thrown enough at her for one evening. He looked at his new watch, announced it was getting on toward one o'clock, and suggested she sleep on it.

Gale agreed. They went back inside; just as they were parting for the night, she stopped him. "King—thank you."

"Oh, you are most welcome," he said.

King got ready for bed quickly, but he had trouble getting to sleep. He was excited; Gale was at least no longer saying no, and that was a big step. King had plunged into an area calling for Dennis Cox's particular brand of expertise, and he'd handled it! He hadn't stuttered or choked up or wheedled; he'd put his proposition to her in straight business terms and had come as close to convincing her as could reasonably be expected at this stage of the game.

Of course she'd want to own half of Keystone Robotics. That was a given. But would she want to own it badly enough to overcome her scruples against weapons? King rather thought she would; being handed half a prosperous business on a silver platter was enough to make anyone reconsider her personal ethics system. Gale was no fool; she'd know when it was time to adjust.

If anybody had told King a year ago that he'd give away half of his business, King would have thought that person was out of his mind. But he needed Gale to keep from losing the weapons platform project, and he couldn't think of anything else that might bring her around. Besides, it was Dennis's half he was giving away, not his own. King made a mental note to call the Pittsburgh lawyer who'd drawn up the original partnership agreement and get things rolling.

King honestly wanted Gale Fredericks as his partner; but beyond that, she was unknowingly a part of his plan to convince the police that he had no reason for wanting Dennis Cox dead. The next time he talked to Sergeant Larch or Malecki—and there would be a next itme, he was sure of that—the next time they spoke, he'd agonize over the impossibility of finding someone with Dennis's precise combination of talents. Gale was the best designer he'd ever worked with, he'd say; she'd designed several complicated machines on her own as well as helped him on his bigger projects. But she lacked Dennis's experience, he'd say, as well as his business acumen. King would make sure the police understood he was wrapped up in worries about the future of his company—worries that would not exist if Dennis Cox were still alive.

That should do it.

Eventually he calmed down to the point where he was starting to get drowsy. The big bed was even more comfortable than the one in his own home; maybe he should get a new one. It would be hard, leaving this apartment; he'd like to live here. And he got a kick out of sharing the place, even though only temporarily, with two attractive married women—one of whom he didn't much like, the other whom he liked perhaps too much. Just thinking about them lying in their beds was enough to give him an erection. Neither woman had ever given King the slightest indication that a middle-of-the-night visit from him would be welcome. But perhaps if he took the initiative . . .

No. King groaned and rolled over. *That* much nerve, he didn't have.

* 9 *

The next day was Sunday. Gale announced she had to get back to Pittsburgh; a new industrial robot she'd worked on was scheduled for demonstration on Monday and she'd already put the client off once.

King nodded. "Also, you need some time to think about my offer. Talk it over with Bill, see what he thinks." King was counting on Husband Bill, who owned his own business, to look at all that extra money that would be coming in and help talk her into it. Unless he was one of those husbands who couldn't stand having wives more successful than they.

"Oh, I already know what Bill will say," Gale smiled. "He'll say go for it. But this is a decision I have to make myself."

King was tempted to tell her to forget about the weapons platform and accept the partnership with no strings attached. Before Dennis and Gregory had died, he would have done just that, blurting it out; now he was learning caution. "What time's your plane?"

It wasn't until late afternoon, so it seemed natural for Gale to sit in when King and Mimi had another go at planning a work schedule. Gale told Mimi she was just there to listen, but she couldn't resist asking questions and making a suggestion or two. Neither of the other two did anything to discourage her.

"It seems pretty clear," King said, "that what defeated the earlier design teams was not the operation of the weapons, but locomotion. Defense wants a platform that'll move over any kind of solid surface, including ice."

"The next generation," Mimi said, "will be amphibious."

"Yeah," King grinned, "and won't that be fun? But right now we don't have to make this thing walk on water. However, half the earth's land mass is impassable by wheels, so that means legs. Legs that move sideways as well as forward and backward. We can make the platform statically stable with six legs, but I'm wondering if that's going to be good enough."

Mimi chewed on the end of her pencil. "This platform, it's going to have to be a self-directed shape-changer."

"Totally self-directed?" Gale asked. "I see problems."

"I know," King sighed. "But the Defense Department wants the soldier-operator to concentrate on battle tactics and not have to worry about flat tires and oil changes. So the platform is going to have to switch means of locomotion by itself, in response to what its own tactile sensors tell it. No outside help."

"Separate programming," Mimi nodded. "But I'll bet they want an override." She shuffled through the papers on the table, looking for the right specifications.

"That's not the biggest problem," King pointed out. "Our main worry is space. We're going to have to find a way to pack all the wheels and legs and treads and whatever into the small amount of room the specs allow us."

"So that's going to have to come first," Gale said. "How big do the wheels have to be? Legs are collapsible, wheels aren't—not dependably so, anyway. But what about treads? This platform's going to be too heavy to do much serious climbing."

"Tell that to the Defense Department," Mimi sniffed. "Steps, hilly terrain—the electromagnetic gun platform stops at nothing."

"Well, the steps won't be a problem," Gale told her. "You could use the technique Quest Technologies developed for their wheelchair that climbs stairs. Sonar sensors to measure the angularity of the steps and then treads substituted for wheels."

King put on a sober expression. "But can it climb ladders?" Mimi slammed down her pencil. "Oh, this is too much! Ladders? Why, the sheer weight of the platform—"

"I was joking, Mimi," King laughed.

They worked steadily for several hours, until King's growling stomach reminded them all they were getting hungry. They decided to grab a bite at JFK; both Mimi and King were beginning to suffer from cabin fever and needed to get out of the apartment for a while, regardless of the police's warnings. Mimi called for the MechoTech limo to come pick them up.

On the way to the airport, Gale and Mimi got into a mild argument about some aspect of the platform's design that they didn't see eye-to-eye on. King was delighted; both women were acting as if it were a settled matter that Gale was now part of the team. He leaned back and closed his eyes, listening to the sound of their voices and not thinking about anything at all. He was happy.

When they pulled into the terminal and the limo driver let them out, King hoisted Gale's carry-all over his shoulder and looked around. Usually he disliked airports; but this one didn't seem especially intimidating, today. He led the way to the nearest restaurant.

They'd barely had time to glance at the menu when a young man who looked like Joe College stepped up to their table and showed them an NYPD badge. "Mrs. Hargrove, Mr. Sarcowicz—you shouldn't be here. It's too exposed. Will you come with me, please?"

Mimi was the first to find her voice. "How did you . . . you *followed* us?"

"Please come with me. We can't protect you here."

We? King looked around and spotted an even younger cop standing at the restaurant's entrance, his eyes x-raying everyone in sight as he attempted to identify potential assassins lurking among the hungry customers. He and Mimi were being watched, followed? "It's a public restaurant," King protested. "Nothing will happen here."

Gale placed her hand on his forearm. "We'd better do as he says." She stood up.

King and Mimi exchanged a glance and somewhat impatiently followed suit. They all three trailed after the young . . . officer? detective?—who stopped just inside the entrance to the restaurant where the second cop was waiting. "You were asked not to leave town," Joe College said to them in a tone of reprimand.

"We're not going anywhere," King replied irritably. "We're just seeing off our friend here."

The second cop pulled out a notebook and asked Gale her name. She gave him a strange look and then took a Keystone Robotics business card out of her shoulder bag. "I work for Mr. Sarcowicz," she said in further explanation.

The young cop glanced at the card and nodded. "Gale Fredericks, right. You just got here yesterday."

"That's right." Wonderingly.

"They checked with the security guards at the apartment building," Mimi murmured.

"You checked on *me*?" Gale asked.

"We check everybody that goes into that apartment. Okay, I think you'd better say goodbye right here. Then we'll escort you two back to your limousine."

Gale's mouth had tightened into a thin line. Her eyes darted back and forth between King and the two policemen, and her breathing became more rapid. "King, I've decided," she said suddenly. "I accept your offer."

His heart skipped a beat. "Which one?"

"Both of them. You shouldn't have to face this alone."

Ah, she'd found her rationale! King let out a whoop and gave her a hug—which embarrassed them both. "That's great, Gale! I'll call the lawyer first thing in the morning."

"I can't get back right away. One of us ought to—"

"I know. Call me tomorrow when you get a breathing space and we'll figure out how to handle everything."

Gale told Mimi goodbye, glanced uncertainly at the police, and went back into the restaurant. "Let's go," Joe College said.

The two youthful policemen marched them back to where the limo driver had parked, a lengthy trek. King didn't mind; he could have floated the whole distance.

Mimi was watching him slyly out of the corner of her eye. "That was fortunate, wasn't it? You know it was our official escort here that tipped the scale in your favor, don't you?"

King grinned at her. "Whatever it takes."

"You're something of an opportunist, aren't you, King? I would never have suspected it."

"Oh, not really. She was already ninety percent hooked on the project—you know she was."

Mimi admitted the truth of that. "Well, I'm glad it's settled. Now we can tell Warren Osterman we're back at full strength again."

Full strength. Oh, yes indeedy. King had never felt stronger in his life.

It took King three tries the following morning to reach his lawyer in Pittsburgh. He told him he wanted to buy Dennis Cox's share of the business, and to start drawing up new partnership papers.

That done, King tried to think what to do next. The unexpected appearance of the police in the airport restaurant the day before had reminded him exactly how seriously the NYPD was taking the supposed threat to his and Mimi's lives. It occurred to him that if he went on acting as if he *knew* he wasn't in danger, they just might change their minds. Things were going too smoothly for him to risk making the police suspicious now.

What would a man do who thought his life was in danger? Never leave the safety of his nest, first of all. But that was only a temporary measure; sooner or later, he'd have to go out. So then what? Hire a bodyguard? Possible, but unpalatable; King just didn't want to put up with the inconvenience. But there had to be something he could do.

His phone conversation with his lawyer in Pittsburgh still lingered in his mind and provided him with the nudge he needed. He'd go see a lawyer. A man who thought he might die suddenly would make a will.

He scouted up a copy of the NYNEX *Yellow Pages* and found nearly fifty pages of lawyers and their advertisements. He looked at the guide of lawyers arranged by practice; under the heading WILLS TRUST & PROBATE ESTATES only about twenty entries were listed. Well, then, which one? He ran his finger down the list and one name jumped out at him: Howard J. M. Liebermann. Now who the hell was Howard Liebermann and why should that one name have stood out from the rest? Howard Liebermann, with two middle initials.

Two middle initials . . . it came back to him. The kid he'd met during one of his stops on Fifty-seventh Street—Ricky, that was his name. Liebermann was the lawyer handling Ricky's father's estate, and the one Ricky suspected of fooling around with his mom. King felt an urge to take a look at this seducer of grieving widows; he called Howard J. M. Liebermann and made an appointment for late that afternoon.

When the time for his appointment approached, he told Mimi what he was going to do and asked if she had made a will; his earlier reluctance to worry her had abated considerably. Mimi's face changed expression about three times, but she said her affairs were in order.

In the limousine on the way to Liebermann's office, King remembered that Monday was the day he was supposed to go back to the hospital for a check-up. But he couldn't very well go when he didn't know which hospital he'd been in. Of course, one telephone call to Rae Borchard would take care of that. Well, perhaps tomorrow. King kept looking through the rear window of the limo, trying to spot the police car that must be following him. No luck. In the movies, "making" a tail was so easy; in the reality of New York traffic, it was impossible.

The suite of offices occupied by Howard J. M. Liebermann and staff reflected a solid if not glamorous practice. Liebermann himself was a surprise; the great Lothario was short, plump, and balding. He had delicate hands that he used gracefully when he talked, showing off the carefully manicured nails. A bit vain, then. But the overall impression the lawyer created was one of stodginess, and King began to suspect that Ricky had been mistaken.

King didn't have to do much explaining. Liebermann knew who he was; he'd read the *Times* account of the two deaths last Thursday and got straight to the nub of the matter. "You think you are in danger, Mr. Sarcowicz?" he asked.

King frowned. "The police think so. At first I was convinced both deaths were just accidents, but now I'm not so sure. Anyway, I figured it wouldn't hurt . . ."

"I understand," the lawyer murmured smoothly. "Everyone should make out a will anyway, whether there's danger or not. Do you have a previous will?"

"No. I can't tell you exactly how much I have to leave, because it changes from week to week. A dollar amount isn't necessary, is it?"

"Not at all. All that's needed is a statement of your intent for the disposition of your property and effects." Liebermann drew a legal pad toward him and started making notes. "How many heirs will there be?"

"Only two. With the exception of a hundred thousand dollars, I want everything I own to go to Gale Fredericks. That includes my business, my house and its contents, and a few investments my partner made for me. My late partner," he amended. Reading upside down, he saw that Liebermann had written down *Gail Fredericks*. "That's g-a-l-e," he told him.

Liebermann raised an eyebrow and made the correction. "Changing times. 'G-a-l-e' used to be a man's name. Her address?"

King gave him the address of Keystone Robotics. "I'll get her home address to you later."

"Fine. And the hundred thousand dollars?"

"I want that to go to Mrs. Rowe, r-o-w-e, my next-door neighbor. She'd going to be having medical expenses and a cash gift will help."

"First name?"

King felt sheepish. He'd lived next door to the old lady for eleven years without ever bothering to learn her first name. "Elvira," he improvised. "No—wait. She once told me that was her middle name. I'll have to get back to you on that."

Liebermann asked for her address and wrote it down. "Well, I see no problems. Call me as soon as you have Ms Fredericks's home address and Mrs. Rowe's first name, and I'll have the will ready for your signature an hour later."

"That's all?"

"That's all. It's a straightforward bequest with no conditions attached. Just don't delay getting the missing information to me."

King said he wouldn't and thanked the lawyer for his help. He was tempted to ask Liebermann what Ricky's last name was and whether the boy was doing all right or not; but even that tenuous a connection to Fifty-seventh Street was something he'd better avoid. When he left the building he paused a moment, to make sure the police saw him coming out. He still couldn't spot them.

He climbed into the limo. King wanted to buy a billfold, but he didn't want a repetition of yesterday's scene at the airport restaurant. He took a fifty-dollar bill from the envelope of cash Gale had brought and asked the limo driver to go into a store for him. All the time the driver was gone, King kept looking around for Joe College or whoever was on duty today. *A man could get paranoid.*

Back at the apartment, with his new billfold containing cash and nothing else, King indulged in a few moments' silent gloating. Someone from the police department was probably in Liebermann's office right then, finding out what King had been doing there. Or, if they truly were protecting him and not checking up on him, he could mention to one of the investigating detectives that he'd just made out his will and Liebermann would be there to back him up. He was covered either way.

But his visit to the lawyer's office had set him to wondering how old Mrs. Rowe was doing. Would she be back home yet? Probably not. So King called Shadyside Hospital in Pittsburgh and made his inquiries. He was told that the old lady had suffered a second stroke Friday morning and had died.

Tuesday was Dennis's funeral. King remembered something he ought to do; he called Gale Fredericks and asked her to find a phone number for Dennis's parents. King had never met them, but they'd think it odd if they didn't hear from him at a time like this.

Mr. Cox took the call. King expressed his condolences and told the older man he couldn't come to the funeral because the police wouldn't let him leave New York. Yes, Mr. Cox said, Mrs. Fredericks had already explained his situation.

That was all right, then.

Early in the afternoon Rae Borchard came to the apartment. By then King and Mimi were in a position to tell her some of what they'd be needing from MechoTech and its contractors. The conference table in the office was covered with papers, lists and graphs and schedules as well as a superb collection of creative doodling. King noticed that Mimi kept sneaking sideways glances at Rae when she thought the other woman wasn't looking; then he remembered that Mimi suspected Rae of being out to kill them all. The best antidote to that nonsense was work.

"One thing, Rae," he said. "I've been studying the specs the earlier design teams worked with, and the weapons systems are different in every case. And in every case the original designs were amended. The last team before us had twenty-seven different weapons modifications they had to accommodate."

"Yes, alas. Defense is always trying to improve on what they've got," Rae stated. "Some of those modifications were quite minor. But the weapons manufacturers are still hard at work building the absolutely perfect, no-fault, wearever electromagnetic gun." Her tone indicated skepticism.

"Meaning they'll be pulling a few switches on us?"

"Meaning exactly that. You're going to have to be flexible."

"Lovely," Mimi said sarcastically. "How can I design a program for weapons that keep changing all the time? Rae, we can't really get going on this until we interface with the people at Army Tactical Command and Control Systems. But they're in Washington, and we can't leave New York. You see the problem?"

Rae nodded, unperturbed by this first roadblock. "Let me see what I can do about getting the mountain to come to Muhammad. They ought to be willing to meet with you here, considering the circumstances."

"And we'll need to see the gun manufacturers as well," King reminded her.

"Yes. If I can't arrange a conference, I'll have a word with our legal department. I don't think the police can force you to stay in New York. MechoTech can always hire bodyguards to go with you."

King leaned back in his chair and clasped his hands behind his head, staring up at a chandelier that bore a suspicious resemblance to the spaceship in *Close Encounters*. "Bodyguards, you say. Rae, we're pretty much stalled until we can talk to those people in Washington. I don't much like the idea of bodyguards, and here at least it's not necessary. The police are keeping an eye on us."

"Aren't they, though?" Mimi told Rae how they'd been followed to JFK on Sunday.

"It's just as well they are following us," King pointed out. "Mimi and I are going batty cooped up like this. We've got to get out."

Rae was adamantly opposed. "No—you mustn't go out. Not yet. Put up with it a while longer. It won't last forever."

King grinned. "At home sometimes I virtually lived in my lab, trying to meet a deadline or working on some problem I couldn't let go of. Talk about cooped up! And you know something? It didn't bother me a bit. Because there I knew I could walk out any time I wanted to. It makes a difference."

"I know it's not pleasant. But surely the police are following you from a distance? How much protection can they give you that way? You can't go out yet."

"King went out yesterday and nothing happened," Mimi said, a little too casually. "Maybe we're making too much of a fuss."

Good old Mimi, King laughed to himself. *Count on her to tattle.* With a show of great reluctance, he allowed Rae to drag it out of him that he'd been to see a lawyer about making his will. That little tidbit cast a satisfying pall on the conversation.

And that was the moment the police chose to arrive.

King let them in. Sergeant Marian Larch and Sergeant Ivan Malecki stood in the entryway, looking grim. "Where's Mimi Hargrove?" Sergeant Larch asked.

"In the office, with Rae Borchard. Why? What's happened?"

"We'll follow you," Sergeant Malecki said pointedly.

King shrugged and led the way. In the office, Malecki told him to sit down. The two police detectives remained standing.

"What is it?" Rae Borchard asked.

"For the last five days," Sergeant Larch told them, "we've been questioning the people who worked on this Defense project before you. We've had the police in four states helping us out. I've been to California myself, and my partner spent two days in Texas. And every single person we contacted said the same thing. They said this weapons platform you're working on is a loser, that there's no way to make it work within the specifications the Defense Department is insisting on."

"Well, of course they'd say that," King snickered. "They failed, after all. The platform's going to be tricky, no question of that—but it's do-able."

"Whether the platform can be made to work or not isn't the point. The point is that all four of the earlier design teams *think* it can't work. Don't you understand? They don't *want* a second go at it."

"And if they don't want another chance," Sergeant Malecki spelled it out for them, "they have no reason to kill off your design team. Got it?"

"They're lying," Mimi stated flatly. "Trying to save face."

"We checked their books," Sergeant Larch told her. "They all took a bath, without exception. The funding that looked so generous at first wasn't enough to keep up with all the changes the government kept making. So every one of them put their own money into it, gambling on winning huge contracts if they could make the damned thing work. But they couldn't."

Malecki was reading from a notebook. "They all said Defense kept adding refinements to the weapons that took up space they needed for other things, like wheels and such. A couple of 'em got additional grant money, but it was never enough. A hell of a lot of money's been wasted on this thing."

His partner nodded. "One of the men I talked to told me his company got so badly stung the first time that now they wouldn't touch the project with a ten-foot Bulgarian. Another company went bankrupt trying to keep up with all the changes and additions. Mrs. Hargrove, Mr. Sarcowicz—none of these people are out to kill you. They don't want anything to do with your electromagnetic gun platform."

King watched woodenly as Mimi and Rae exchanged puzzled looks. Mimi swallowed and said, "Then Gregory and Dennis . . . are you saying their deaths were accidents after all?"

Malecki snorted. "No way."

"Then what—"

"Mrs. Hargrove," Marian Larch said firmly. "Four people were staying in that apartment. Two of them died at the same time under circumstances that can only be called bizarre. The other two were ostensibly out of the apartment at the time, and both have alibis that have gaping holes in them. You say you were on your way back from the airport when the two deaths occurred, and there's no way of proving that. Mr. Sarcowicz says he was wandering the streets until the muggers got him in the park. Since neither—"

"Now wait a minute!" Mimi cried, her voice high. "What exactly are you saying?"

The detective looked back and forth between Mimi and King. "I thought it was clear. What we're saying is that Gregory Dillard and Dennis Cox were killed by one of you two."

King sat at the poker table in the apartment's games room, his chin sunk on his chest and his arms folded. The games room also had a billiards table, but right then it was in shadow. The room's only illumination came from a lamp suspended from the ceiling, spilling a pool of light directly on to the poker table and him—*just like an old-timey police station*, King thought in irritation.

Across from him and just far enough back from the table to be out of the pool of light sat Marian Larch. Ivan Malecki had stayed in the office with Mimi, where he was undoubtedly giving her the third degree or whatever it was called nowadays. Rae Borchard had delivered a blistering denunciation of police methods before rushing off to notify Warren Osterman and get them a lawyer and do whatever else she could think to do.

"Five days," said Sergeant Larch out of the shadow, "we've wasted five whole days. Around here it's a rule of thumb that if you don't crack a homicide in three days, chances are good your perp will walk. And we just spent *five days* on a wild goose chase."

King felt she was waiting for him to say something. "Is that my fault?" he asked in a tone of injured innocence.

"Yours or Mimi's. You want Mimi to take the blame for something you did?"

"I never murdered anyone. And neither did Mimi—you're on the wrong track."

"With Dennis Cox out of the way, now you've got Keystone Robotics all to yourself. Was that your motive—plain old greed?"

"Dammit, Sergeant, you couldn't be more wrong! I *needed* Dennis—I can't run Keystone by myself! And I'm not even going to try. I've already got a new partner."

"Who?"

"Gale Fredericks. You met her . . . ah, Saturday."

"Uh-huh. So it's all set, is it." Not buying it.

"It's in the works. I called my lawyer on Monday and instructed him to draw up new partnership papers. You can check with him."

"Oh, that's a good idea." Only lightly sarcastic. Marian Larch leaned into the circle of light with a pen and notebook in her hands. "Name?"

King told her the lawyer's name and watched her write it down.

"Not Howard J. M. Liebermann?"

Ah, so she did know about the will. "No, my lawyer in Pittsburgh," he said, thinking this was as good an opening as any. "Gale's going to be working on the project. I know she can handle that, I'm sure of it."

The sergeant picked up her cue. "Meaning you're not sure she can handle Keystone? Why'd you make her a partner if you're unsure of her?"

King sighed, deeply. "Sergeant Larch, Gale Fredericks is the best young designer I know—she's already better than Dennis Cox ever was, and I can't think of anyone I'd rather have working with me. But she doesn't have Dennis's experience." He went on to explain about Dennis's unique combination of talents, his hands-on experience in robot design that meshed with a superior business sense to make him an ideal partner. He said it was a combination he knew of in no other person. "Gale and I may end up hiring someone to manage Keystone for us, but first we want to try it without having to rely on an outsider to keep us solvent. So you see, Sergeant, I don't profit from my partner's death. In fact, it's going to work a hardship on me."

She asked questions. She wanted to know financial details, and King gave them to her as fully and as honestly as he could. He knew once she checked into them, she'd find Dennis's death was costing him money—the amount he had to put up to buy his dead partner's share of the business before he signed it over to Gale for the token sum of one dollar. He would come out looking like a white knight valiantly struggling to save his business.

Or maybe not. "You and Gale Fredericks," Sergeant Larch said, "you got something going, have you?"

King felt his face tighten up in annoyance. "No, we do not have 'something going'."

"You're giving her half your business. Half of Keystone Robotics is going to a partner who can't pay for it. You don't run into that kind of generosity very often."

"I *need* Gale—the same way I needed Dennis. Can't you understand that?"

"Dennis might have been in the way. You get rid of him, there's room for Gale."

"Sergeant, you have a nasty and suspicious mind."

"I'm paid to be suspicious. And nasty too, come to think of it." The grilling went on—about his plans for Keystone, his plans for the weapons platform, about his movements on the day Dennis and Gregory had died. She asked what he thought of the other members of the team; in an only slightly exaggerated display of openness, King let her know that while he and Mimi had once been at odds in the past, he'd never had any reason to dislike Gregory Dillard. Or want him dead.

But it took a lot to satisfy Sergeant Marian Larch. She leaned on him hard, questioning every little remark he made. She hinted the police were unimpressed by the theory that Gregory had been lured into leaning out the window by a one-footed pigeon. She hinted at conspiracy, at the possibility that King and Mimi were in it together. She came back to Gale and told him that if they were lovers, the Pittsburgh police would find it out for her. Then she wanted to know if he and Mimi were lovers. And then, god help him, she wanted to know if he and *Dennis* had been lovers.

In two hours the only break she allowed him was five minutes to go to the bathroom. The interrogation ended only when Rae Borchard showed up with a MechoTech lawyer in tow. The lawyer, obviously comfortable only with corporate law, solemnly warned both King and Mimi not to talk to the police until they could get a criminal lawyer to advise them. Mimi and King exchanged a sour look; it was a little late for that. But neither Marian Larch nor Ivan Malecki argued the point; King had the feeling they'd accomplished what they came there to accomplish—which was the simple intimidating of their two suspects.

Sergeant Larch smiled sweetly at King as she left. "See you tomorrow," she purred.

When they were gone, and the MechoTech lawyer as well, Rae Borchard said, "Don't talk to her, King. Or to the other one, either. I don't know what they could be thinking of—this is terrible."

Mimi looked exhausted. "I've never had anyone say things to me like that in my life. That Sergeant Malecki accused me of sleeping with both Gregory and Dennis, of trying to get rid of my SmartSoft partners, of—"

"I don't know what you're worried about," King snapped, his temper frayed. "They have eight witnesses who saw a *man* standing at the apartment window when it happened."

"But only one of them thought to count the floors," Mimi answered mournfully, "and now that one's saying he's not sure he counted right."

"What?"

"That's what Sergeant Malecki told me. There may not have been any third man in that apartment at all."

"Oh . . . I didn't know that. Somehow Sergeant Larch neglected to mention that little fact."

Mimi sniffed disconsolately. "So now the police are thinking the killer could have been either a woman or a man. They're thinking it could have been me."

"Don't talk to them," Rae repeated. "Either of you."

So the floor-counting witness was having second thoughts, King mused. Well, well . . . wasn't that interesting. Now the police were thinking it could very well have been Mimi who killed Dennis and Gregory. Why not? King liked that.

It could have been *Mimi.*

* 10 *

King fully expected to find Marian Larch camped on his doorstep the next morning, but she wasn't there. Nor was the other one, Ivan Malecki—much to Mimi's relief. Rae Borchard had set up a ten o'clock appointment for them with a criminal lawyer; with luck, they could avoid the police all morning.

Since King's and Mimi's status had changed from potential victims to that of murder suspects, the police's earlier instruction that they stay in the apartment for their own protection was tacitly lifted. Mimi was nervous about venturing away from the safety of the apartment building, though; King had to talk her into going out for breakfast. Their behavior had to be the same; it would set the police to wondering if she acted afraid and he didn't.

"They're bound to be following us," Mimi said as they turned on to Fifth Avenue.

"I know." King was counting on their following, on their seeing that neither of their suspects was afraid to be alone with the other.

They chose a coffee shop at random off Fifth Avenue and slid into the only empty booth. A waitress appeared, shooting covert glances at King's face. His bruises had faded considerably, but he was still marked up enough to attract attention; their waitress, who was very young, was having trouble not staring. King ordered fruit juice and coffee and pancakes and sausages, but Mimi wanted only tea and a glass of tonic water. "Queasy this morning," she explained.

They sat in glum silence until the waitress brought their orders, determinedly not looking at King. King polished off his breakfast quickly and wiped his mouth. "Mimi, we have to talk."

She just looked at him, not even trying to hide her depression.

"The police are wrong. I know I didn't kill Dennis and Gregory—and I sure as hell don't think you did. Larch and Malecki are way off base."

"Rae Borchard."

"She didn't kill them either. *Nobody* killed them, Mimi. It was just two freak accidents—tragic and stupid, but still accidents. And if the police weren't so conditioned to looking for homicides under every bush, they'd see both deaths were accidents."

"Speaking of," Mimi said, staring over his shoulder.

King turned to see their two police detectives approaching their table. He groaned as Marian Larch sat down next to him and said, "Move over, King—you're taking up too much room." Ivan Malecki slid in next to Mimi and asked the waitress to bring them coffee.

"Can't we even have breakfast without being harassed?" King complained.

"What harrassed?" the woman next to him said. "We're just having coffee with you."

"We don't have to talk to you!" Mimi said defiantly.

Sergeant Larch looked at her partner in mock resignation. "Why do they always say that?"

Sergeant Malecki made a face. "They hear it on TV alla time," he answered with a long-suffering air.

"Well, she's right," King grumbled. "We *don't* have to talk to you. In fact, we're on our way to see our lawyer."

"Howard J. M. Liebermann?" Sergeant Larch asked innocently.

That was the second time she'd mentioned him; she'd brought his name up yesterday as well. "No, a criminal lawyer. Why I went to see Liebermann is my own business."

"You made out your will," Malecki said.

Bingo! King made a show of being angry. "You've been checking up on me."

"We always check up on people we think are killers."

"Don't be idiotic!" Mimi snapped. "If he's worried enough to make out a will, then he's not a killer!"

Ah, Mimi, I love you!

"Unless that's just what he wants us to think," Sergeant Larch remarked.

But Marian, I'm none too fond of you.

"What about you?" Sergeant Malecki asked Mimi. "Why didn't you make out a will too?"

"I already have a will," Mimi said through clenched teeth.

The young waitress showed up with coffee, and this time King caught her sneaking a peek at him. She turned pink and laughed. "What's the other guy look like?"

"Not a scratch on him," King answered, a little put out. "A Sumo wrestler beat me up when I wouldn't give him my seat on the subway."

She frowned, believing him. "How can people get away with things like that?"

King jerked a thumb in Marian Larch's direction. "Ask her. She's a detective."

"Really?" The waitress's face lit up. "You're a private investigator?"

"A public investigator," Marian Larch said. "NYPD."

The waitress looked disappointed. When she'd gone, Sergeants Larch and Malecki started a lively conversation about the current state of professional wrestling; they gave it their full attention, effectively excluding King and Mimi. When they'd finished their coffee, the two detectives smiled cheerfully, said goodbye, and left.

Mimi looked astonished. "Now what was that all about?"

"They're just letting us know they're around," King said. "I have a feeling we're going to be seeing a lot of those two."

She made a gesture of annoyance—and knocked over King's glass that still had an inch of fruit juice in it. King jerked sideways in the booth to escape the juice that spilled over the tabletop in his direction.

"Oh! Did it get on you?"

"Just a drop. Most of it went on the seat."

"Oh, where is that waitress?" Mimi was embarrassed. "Here, use this." She handed him a paper napkin and started dabbing at the table with another one.

King dipped the napkin in his water glass and rubbed at the small spot on his jacket sleeve. "Don't worry about it, Mimi. I do that sort of thing all the time."

The young waitress showed up with a sponge; King apologized for the mess and left her a big tip. He and Mimi went out of the coffee shop and paused a moment to get their bearings. *I do that sort of thing all the time.* It dawned on King that he hadn't spilled anything or dropped anything or broken anything in almost a week. He hadn't bumped into anybody, and he hadn't stepped on anyone's foot.

"Excuse you," he said to a burly fellow who'd just bumped into *him*. The man didn't even look back.

King and Mimi set out for the lawyer's office, five blocks farther downtown on Fifth. The short walk did them both good; they'd been cooped up too long. Mimi stopped looking back over her shoulder and even smiled once or twice.

Their session with the criminal lawyer, whose name was Banks, was tedious and ultimately not very helpful. Banks had taken them both through their accounts of where they were and what they'd been doing at the time Dennis Cox and Gregory Dillard had died. He wanted to know if they could produce witnesses. He wanted to know if the police had any reason to suspect some sort of hanky-panky had been going on among the four of them, either financial or sexual. He wanted to know how MechoTech's proposed mergers with Keystone and SmartSoft would change their lives. He wanted to know everything.

An hour later the session had ended, and King felt as if he'd been through a wringer. He and Mimi rode the elevator down in silence; when they were back out on the street, an odd moment of awkwardness occurred between them. They looked at each other at the same instant, nodded self-consciously . . . and took off in opposite directions. They'd had enough of each other's company for a while.

On impulse, King climbed aboard the first bus that came along. He slumped into a seat and stared unseeing out the window. Banks had been merciless in his questioning, undoubtedly giving them a foretaste of what they could expect if the matter ever came to trial. To trial! Everything had been going so well; the police had given no indication they suspected him of being involved in Dennis's and Gregory's deaths and were even "protecting" him from some nonexistent killer they were convinced was crouched out there somewhere just waiting for a chance to pounce. And Gale had come around, god bless her! She'd be a better partner than Dennis ever was, and she'd never think of selling him out. Things had been looking *so good*.

This time yesterday King had thought he was virtually home free; yet today he had a fifty-fifty chance of being arrested for murder. Banks had seemed to think the police wouldn't seriously consider a charge of conspiracy, on the basis that if King and Mimi had been in it together they would have alibied each other for the crucial time period.

The advice Banks gave them had been simple: *Keep your mouths shut.* Marian Larch—was she driving along behind the bus even then? Did sergeants do that kind of donkey work? Malecki must be following Mimi, unless the two detectives had decided to switch suspects. King snorted; he was beginning to think of Marian Larch as "his" cop. But the police had no way of knowing whether it was King or Mimi who was responsible for Dennis's and Gregory's deaths; it would be a coin toss as far as they were concerned.

Unless . . . unless they were given some reason to think King was innocent. But if they thought he was innocent, then they'd think Mimi was guilty.

But what would Mimi have to gain by killing Gregory Dillard? She wasn't left in sole control of their business; she still had three other partners. Ah, but now Mimi was the *senior* partner, she'd said. Perhaps some sort of internal power struggle going on at SmartSoft that nobody was talking about? King was trying to think the way he imagined the police would think, trying to see what kind of case they might build against Mimi Hargrove. Money, power, control—a reliable standby in the field of criminal motives that the police would never question.

Yet it wouldn't account for her killing Dennis Cox. To get rid of a witness? Hardly, since he was in the bathtub watching television at the time the window fell on Gregory's neck. Some other reason, then. King thought again of Dennis's hand in Mimi's lap under cover of the conference table at MechoTech; something there? Both the police and their new lawyer had asked questions about sexual goings-on. Mimi made such a big thing of being committed to her marriage, as if that proved how wonderful she was, how she was not afraid to undertake long-term relationships or whatever the yuppie standard of achievement was this year. Say Dennis wanted her to leave her husband Michael; that would spoil the pretty picture she was painting of herself. In that case both King's partner and her own could be seen as posing a threat to her—Gregory professionally and Dennis personally. And the quickest way to end the threats was to get rid of the threateners.

Yeah.

King became aware that most of the people on the bus were getting off; he followed the crowd and found himself in Washington Square. What was he doing here? *Well,* he thought, *why not here?* He didn't have anyplace else to go.

He stopped for a moment to watch a sidewalk artist doing Jesus in pastels and then wandered into the park. A would-be comedian was trying out his material on a small, mostly agreeable crowd; King listened a while and then ambled on. He stayed away from the spot where two guys with acoustic guitars were holding forth, but he dropped a five into the shoe box placed on the ground by the kids breakdancing on roller skates. He found a bench near to where a fire-eater was doing his thing and sat down.

After a while the tensions of the morning began to ease away. Mimi could be made to appear guilty. And that's all it would take to divert attention away from him—the appearance of guilt. They could never prove anything against her.

"Quite a show, isn't it?" a familiar voice asked.

King groaned; he hadn't even seen her sit down. "What do you want, Sergeant Larch?"

"I've always wondered how they do that," she said, gesturing toward the fire-eater. "More than that, I wonder why anyone would *want* to do that. There must be easier ways to attract attention."

"Twice in one day, Sergeant. This has got to be harassment."

She dipped into her shoulder bag for a Kleenex and wiped her nose. "I'm not here to harass you, King. What I want is your help."

He glared at her suspiciously. "How can *I* help?"

"By telling me everything you know about Mimi Hargrove."

"That won't take long. I've never worked with her before."

"How did she and Gregory Dillard get along?"

"Fine, as far as I could tell. It's a little hard to know about Gregory. He was always . . . acting, you know what I mean? He had a very obvious social and business persona that he put on every time I talked to him. The face behind the mask—well, I never saw it."

"And Mimi?"

King was silent for a moment. *Keep your mouth shut*, the lawyer had said. But this was just too good an opportunity. "I used to think Mimi was exactly what she appeared to be. Now I feel I don't really know anybody anymore."

"What does she appear to be?"

"Efficient. Ambitious. Humorless. A bit literal-minded."

"Ambitious, you say. How ambitious? Enough to kill someone who got in her way?"

"Oh, now, look—"

"Come on, King, tell me. Is she ambitious enough to kill?"

What was all this King business? Whatever happened to Mr. Sarcowicz? "I really don't know, *Marian*. How can I answer a question like that? Two days ago I would have said absolutely not. But now that you're so damned sure one of us killed Dennis and Gregory, and I know *I* didn't . . ." He didn't finish the sentence.

"Then it had to be Mimi," she finished for him.

He didn't contradict her. They sat without speaking for a while, just watching the other people in Washington Square Park. King noticed that quite a few of those people were brown-bagging it, and his stomach growled in automatic response.

"Me too," said Marian Larch. "You like Tex-Mex?"
"Uh, yeah, I guess so."
"Cottonwood Café, then. Let's go."
King reluctantly followed her out of the park. He didn't want to sit down to a meal with this police detective; she was up to something and he couldn't figure out what. He waited until they'd walked a couple of blocks and made one final show of protest. "I think you're wrong about Mimi. As weird as the whole thing is, I have to think both Dennis and Gregory died by accident."

She didn't hesitate. "Both those men died with someone else's help. You can be sure of that."

"You're absolutely certain?"

"Absolutely."

King said no more.

The Cottonwood Café was on Bleecker Street. The place was crowded, but not absurdly so; they waited only five minutes for a table. On Marian Larch's recommendation, King ordered a margarita and liked it so much he ordered another one. Starting on his third he told her to order for both of them. She rolled off a bunch of Spanish words he couldn't understand.

"What was all that?" he asked, noticing he was slurring his words.

"Beef and chicken, one order of each. We can split."

When the food came, the waitress set down another margarita in front of him; he didn't remember ordering another but raised no objection to its being there. There was some movement of food between his plate and Marian Larch's; when all the activity stopped, he picked up his fork and dug in. "Marian, this is delish . . . shus!" He ordered another drink.

She smiled. "Glad you like it."

By the time he'd finished his newest margarita, he couldn't tell the beef from the chicken. But he knew whatever he was eating was *good*. And his lunch companion was being good too; she hadn't said a word about Mimi or MechoTech or murder. "The three *Ms*," he mumbled.

"What?"

"Mimi, MechoTech, and murder," he overarticulated, realizing he was sailing a forgotten number of sheets to the wind. "And a fourth *M*. M for Marian."

"I think we'd better get some coffee in you. Otherwise you'll accuse me of getting you drunk on purpose. Then I'll drive you home."

"Home. Pittsburgh?"

Marian laughed. "Sorry." She told the waitress to bring a pot of coffee.

The coffee was scalding hot when it came; he sipped at it gingerly. "You're going to take me back to the apartment? Aren't you afraid that Mimi might kill me? Or I might kill her?"

"Not a chance. Why do you think we told you both that you were our only suspects? It was the best protection we could think of, for whichever one of you is innocent. If Mimi's the killer, she won't dare touch you now. You're safe."

"You're sure of that."

"Drink your coffee.'"

He managed to get two cups down but then protested he was in danger of floating away. Marian paid the bill, left a tip, got King to his feet, and steered him toward the door. Where they stopped; the skies had opened up while they were eating and now it was pouring down.

"It's raining," King remarked perceptively.

"So it is. You wait here while I go get the car." She looked at him weaving on his feet and changed her mind. "On second thought, a little rain in the face might do you good. Come on."

The rain pounding down was cold, far too cold for May. Within minutes both of them were soaked through. The sidewalks had quickly emptied; they saw only two or three other people running for their cars or a taxi. Marian's car, unfortunately, was blocks away. King staggered along as best he could, his teeth chattering. But his head did seem to be clearing up some; his sense of balance improved. *What am I doing here?* he thought. Half-drunk, cold, wet, getting dragged through the streets of the Village by a New York police detective—who at least half suspected him of murder. *And all I wanted to do was design an electromagnetic gun platform.*

By the time they reached the car he was fully sober and miserable. They sat dripping water on the seats while Marian Larch tried to get the defroster to unsteam the windows. The drive back to the apartment was a silent one, broken only by the detective's occasional muttered comments about all the lunatic drivers out that day. King didn't remember inviting her up to dry off, but the next thing he knew she was asking to borrow a bathrobe.

He gave her one, and quickly changed into dry clothes himself. They'd found the apartment empty; Mimi must be off with Sergeant Malecki somewhere. King was still toweling his head dry when he found Marian in a small laundry room off the kitchen, putting her clothes into the dryer. On top of the dryer lay a holstered gun. She saw him looking at it and slipped it into a pocket of the robe she'd borrowed. "Something hot to drink?" she suggested.

King found a box of tea bags and put the water on to heat. The rain pounded against the windowpanes; the day had turned dark and ominous-looking. He switched on the lights, and the kitchen was bathed in a pleasant glow that gave it the look and feel of a warm haven against the storm. It could almost be a cozy domestic scene, if his woman companion were anyone other than a police detective trying to pin a murder rap on him.

"Catch the water right before it boils," Marian said from the stove. "That makes the best tea." He hadn't heard her come in.

They sat at a butcher block table, drinking their tea and listening to the rain. King was beginning to feel human again.

"What did you have to do to get appointed head of this gun platform project?" she asked out of the blue.

Startled, King replied, "I didn't have to do anything. Warren Osterman made the decision."

"You must have lobbied for it, some."

"Nope. The project had to be headed by a designer, so that eliminated Mimi and Gregory right there."

"Mimi and Gregory didn't think so," she interrupted. "They didn't consider themselves eliminated at all. In fact, all four of you wanted to head up this project. You wanted it bad."

How did she know that? "Rae Borchard," he guessed.

The sergeant smiled wryly. "Rae Borchard wouldn't give us the time of day. No, it was Warren Osterman who told us."

"Warren!" King was surprised.

"Relax, he's on your side. It took us forever to convince him that no rival company is out to kill off your entire design team—but once he accepted that, he immediately assumed that Mimi was the culprit. He said you had such a bad case of the clumsies that you might bump somebody off by accident, but you could never execute a successful double murder. You'd find some way to botch it."

"That's nice of him," King said sarcastically, half pleased, half resentful.

"Osterman also said Mimi didn't take your appointment as project leader at all well."

King lowered his head so she couldn't see the expression on his face. "That's true, she didn't."

"He said she went right on campaigning for the job even after he'd announced you'd be in charge. And do you know *how* she campaigned for the job?"

"Probably by badmouthing me."

"That's about it." Marian picked up their cups and took them to the sink. "She's not your friend, King. That doesn't make her a murderer, but watch your back all the same. If she is a murderer, she must have gone back to that other apartment expecting to find all three of you there—the man who had the job she wanted and two others who could keep her from getting it. Does that fit the picture of the Mimi you know?"

He took his time answering. "She's very ambitious," he said with what he hoped was the proper degree of hesitancy.

Marian snorted. "So's Rae Borchard. Hell, *I'm* ambitious. But is Mimi *obsessed*?"

"I'm not qualified to judge obsession," he replied primly, and then slipped in the zinger he'd been saving. "You know she's senior partner of SmartSoft now?"

Marian's eyebrows raised. "No, I didn't. I knew she wasn't the sole owner, but I just assumed they were all equal partners. We slipped up there. Well, well."

King said no more, satisfied for the moment with the climate of doubt he'd contributed to.

Abruptly Marian changed the subject and asked to be shown the rest of the apartment. She'd already seen the games room, with its poker and billiards tables, so King took her into the media room. King liked the media room. He waved an arm expansively and said, "What do you think?"

One wall of the room had four TV screens, a fifty-one-inch projection set at the center and three seventeen-inch screens on top. Shelves containing video equipment were attached to another wall; King pointed out four VCRs, two laser disc players, a satellite receiver. The opposite wall held audio equipment—three each of tuners, integrated amplifiers, audiocassette decks, CD players. And one turntable.

"Overkill?" Marian suggested.

King ignored that and said, "This room has five pairs of speakers built into the walls. And it has a digital sound field processor—you know what that does?"

"No, what?"

"It imitates the acoustics of concert halls and opera houses and the like." He put a disc into the player. "Balcony or orchestra?"

Marian shrugged. "Balcony." An overture to an opera started playing, and the music did sound as if it were coming from an orchestra pit on a building level lower than theirs.

"Now let's move you downstairs." The music was suddenly coming from the same level, and it sounded closer. "Isn't that great?"

"Yeah, it is."

"And look here." King stopped the CD and opened the door of a walk-in closet that had been converted to a video tape library. "Suction fans to eliminate dust. Low-level humidity, constant temperature." He ran his eye over the titles of some of the tapes stored there. "Do you like *Aliens*?"

There was a pause. "I don't believe I've ever met any," Marian replied politely.

King was actually starting to explain when he realized she must have known he meant the movie. She was pulling his leg, needling him? Why? Her face gave nothing away. King didn't like being kidded, especially by this cop who had suddenly appeared out of nowhere to play such a big role in his life, and who now sat listening placidly while he babbled on about mechanized puppets. "They even have articulated lips," he finished lamely.

"Articulated lips, huh?" Marian said absently and waved a hand toward the television screens. "So you can watch *Aliens* and three other movies at the same time here? Or four TV channels?"

"Oh, better than that." He plopped down on a leather chair next to a control unit. "Would you believe thirty-six?"

She perched on the arm of his chair. "Right now, I think I would. What's that thing? Don't you use remote control units?"

King was pressing buttons. "Each of these screens can show nine different PIP freeze-frames, and switching from one signal to another on four separate monitors can get hairy. Even a unified remote can handle only so much. This 'thing' here is a teletext system with a touch screen. Watch." The control unit's screen showed an image of all four monitors; King touched the first one and the screen immediately changed to a numeric keypad. King started entering channel numbers, and after a while thirty-six different pictures were displayed on the four monitors, nine to a screen. "There you have it. Couch potato heaven."

Marian laughed at the sight, enjoying the absurdity of it. She studied the various pictures, counting. "Twelve of those thirty-six channels are broadcasting a show or a movie about crime. Do you think that's a fair sample—one-third of our entertainment is about crime?"

"Did you count the news?"

"No."

"Then make it thirteen out of thirty-six—there's always something about crime on the news."

"Speaking of which, did you notice that you haven't been hounded by news reporters?"

He hadn't, but thought it politic not to say so. "I was wondering about that."

"It's because you and Mimi stayed in this apartment the whole time you were hot news. I suggest you give the security men downstairs a big tip—they did a hell of a job turning away reporters for you."

King hadn't even thought of that. "Does that mean we're no longer, er, hot news?"

"Did anyone accost you today when you went out?"

"Only you."

"The murder of Dennis Cox and Gregory Dillard is last week's news. The reporters probably won't bother you at all now—unless something more happens."

"Something more? What else could happen?"

Marian eased off the chair arm where she'd been perched and stepped around to face King. That placed her squarely in front of the big screen, with its plethora of action going on around her: Victoria Barkley drove a team of horses directly over the sergeant's head. "What else could happen? Mimi could confess. *You* could confess."

"Me! You still think I . . . that's crazy!"

"You're sure Mimi did it?"

"I'm not *sure*—"

"But you think she did?" Captain Kirk scowled at King over Marian's right shoulder.

"Well, if you're convinced it was one of the two of us and I—"

"Yet you don't mind sharing an apartment with someone who might have wanted to kill you?"

"But you said she wouldn't dare try anything now! You said I was safe!"

"And if I said the moon was Roquefort, you'd buy that too? *Why aren't you afraid, King?*"

He swallowed hard. "I . . . I guess that on some level I'm just not convinced that Mimi is a killer." It was the best answer he could come up with.

Marshal Dillon pointed a gun at Marian's left ear. She sighed and said, "That leaves you. Are you a killer, King?"

"*No!*" He was sweating; what kind of game was she playing? Disoriented by all the images in front of him as much as by the questions Sergeant Marian Larch was hurling at him, King jumped up out of his chair and bolted from the media room. He headed toward the living room's balcony; but the rain was still pouring down, so he stood inside and looked out, fidgeting, uncomfortable.

Marian came up to stand next to him. "You're now rid of a partner you didn't really like, and you've got yourself a new one that you do like. Dennis wanted to head your project, and so did Gregory. And so does Mimi. I hope nothing happens to Mimi, King. I really do hope that."

"Nothing is going to happen to Mimi!" he growled. "Why would I want her dead? I already *have* control of the project!"

Marian smiled sadly. "Killers don't always act to get something. Sometimes people kill to protect what they've already got."

"And you think that's what I've done."

"I think my clothes should be dry by now." Without another word, she turned and left.

King was startled at the way she'd broken off the accusations, as abruptly as she'd introduced them. Was that her technique, hit and run? Here he'd been rather pleased with himself for the subtle way he *thought* he'd been casting doubt on the matter of Mimi's innocence . . . was that the problem? Had he been too subtle? Was Marian Larch the kind of cop you had to hit over the head before you could get her attention?

When she came back in, she was dressed in her own clothes. Her shoes were still wet; King hoped they were ruined. "I left your robe in the laundry room," she said. "Thanks for lending it to me. I'm supposed to report to the captain in half an hour, so I'll be going now. Next time you can tell me all about articulated lips." With a cheery wave she was gone.

King sank down to the floor, right where he was standing. Marian Larch was making him *very* uneasy. The other sergeant, Malecki, was probably working the same game on Mimi. He leaned against the glass door to the balcony, trying to get his thoughts in order; he stayed there until his back began to get cold.

He didn't want to think about Marian Larch and her awkward questions, so he went into the office and turned on one of the computers. He couldn't do any real designing until he'd talked to the weapons people in Washington; but perhaps he could get a start on squeezing all those treads and legs into an impossibly small space. He fiddled around for an hour and then gave up; he couldn't concentrate.

Mimi still hadn't come back. Hinting that Mimi Hargrove might not be the innocent she appeared just wasn't going to do the trick. Something more definite, more damning, was called for. Something that would turn the police's attention away from him once and for all.

Yes, something was going to have to be done about Mimi.

* 11 *

King was waiting in Warren Osterman's MechoTech office when the older man came in the following morning. "Hello, King—something up?" Osterman lowered himself cautiously into his leather desk chair and watched the other man pacing aimlessly about the room.

"A couple of things," King said, ignoring any pretense of amenities. "First, just how much patience does Defense have? If we don't get going on this thing—"

"We still have some time. Rae's been trying to arrange a confab, but about half the people you'll need to talk to aren't in Washington right now. And everybody agrees a phone conference won't do the trick. My advice is to let it ride until *they* start requesting a meeting." Osterman took out a handkerchief and blew his nose. "You know how it is with government people—everything is urgent and therefore nothing is."

King nodded without pausing in his pacing. "That's just as well. Warren, every other team that's tried an EM gun platform design failed for the same reason—because Defense kept adding refinements that took up space needed for other things, important things. A mechanism for changing wheels to treads to legs and back again, for instance. There's no way in the world to fit one into the puny amount of space they've allotted for the job. And that space is going to shrink even more. They're going to keep adding things to our design just the way they did to the others."

"I know, but what can you do?"

"We can anticipate them. We can go in saying the whole gun platform has to be bigger. Then we can reserve space for whatever they throw at us later."

"But how much reserve space? You don't know what the next innovation will be."

"I can guess. I'll bet you next year's tax refund that sooner or later they're going to ask us to include launch apparatus for the new earth-penetrating missiles."

Osterman hooted. "Not a chance! Good god, that's an entirely different weapons system. Besides, those missiles are *huge*—"

"I don't mean those big ones that go after underground bunkers and the like." King stopped pacing and stood in front of Osterman's desk. "But smaller ones, the size of rifle-launched missiles—think of the damage they could do! They could take out gas mains, underground power lines. That weapons system *is* different, but sooner or later it's going to dawn on someone in Washington that small earth-penetrators are a natural auxiliary to the electromagnetic gun."

Osterman looked interested. "So what do you have in mind?"

King sat down in a chair facing the desk and took a deep breath. "I say we beat 'em to the punch. We go in and suggest it ourselves. Once Defense is convinced that the EM gun and the earth-penetrators belong together, they'll have to approve a larger platform—and that's where we'll get the extra space we need for changing the modes of locomotion. It's the only way we can lick this thing."

Warren Osterman was silent for a long while, and then his face gradually crinkled into a big smile. "By god, that's devious! Tell the military they need more weapons. Oh, how they'll love that! Ha!"

King grinned. "Thought you'd like it. It should get us off the hook quite nicely."

"It's too early to start posing for statues," the older man grinned back. "We still have to pull it off."

They talked details for a while and agreed to go ahead with the plan. Then Osterman said, "You know, King, you've changed. I used to wonder who tied your shoelaces for you, but no more. You never would have thought up a move like this before. Dennis Cox might have, but not you."

"Maybe that was the problem. I depended too much on Dennis."

Osterman agreed. "He depended on you to develop the innovative technology, and you depended on him to take care of the business end for you. You complemented each other, but each of you reinforced the other's weak spots. When was the last time Dennis came up with a truly original design?"

King smiled ruefully. "I can't remember."

Osterman hesitated. "This new partner of yours. Is she . . ."

"Original. And quick. And willing to clean up after me only to a point, I suspect. She's no Dennis, that's certain."

The older man nodded, reassured. "It's a horrible thing to think, but you're probably better off without Dennis. If the police ever decide to arrest Mimi, that is."

King got up and started pacing again. "That's the other thing I wanted to talk to you about. Warren—why did you tell the police the other three all wanted my job?"

Osterman's face took on a pained look. "They were looking for a motive. Once the police told me the killer had to be you or Mimi . . . well. I knew it couldn't be you—you're just not mean-spirited enough to go out and kill someone. So it has to be Mimi, and she probably is capable of killing. I thought if I told them about the competition for your job, I'd help head them in the right direction."

King managed a smile; the old man had been trying to protect him. "Thanks, Warren. Unfortunately, it didn't work. Sergeant Larch made a point of telling me that sometimes people kill to protect what they have, not just to gain something more. I'm still a suspect."

Osterman groaned.

"And there's something else. If Mimi did kill Dennis and Gregory, are we supposed to go on working with her as if nothing has happened? How do you think I feel, right there in the apartment with her?"

"Things were rough this morning?"

"She was still asleep when I left. She didn't get in until late."

"Do you want to move back to the other apartment? Or into a hotel?"

King made a show of considering the suggestion. "That might not be a bad idea. Let me think about it."

They had nothing more to talk about, so King left. Without knowing it, Warren Osterman had put his finger on a problem that King could find no immediate solution for. It would be a good move toward convincing the police of his innocence if he left the apartment for a hotel; it would look as if he were afraid to stay alone with Mimi. But at the same time, he didn't want to separate himself from the police's only other suspect. If he were going to come up with a plan for directing suspicion toward her, he wanted her where he could get at her. What worried him was the possibility that *Mimi* might move to a hotel. He'd been trying to think of a way to persuade her to stay but so far had come up empty.

King stopped in Rae Borchard's office and invited her to have lunch with him.

Warren Osterman had been right about one thing, King thought; he *had* changed, a little. He was noticing more, paying better attention. He'd had to watch various people carefully to see how his story was going over; he thought he knew every facial expression in Marian Larch's repertoire, for instance. And even though circumstances had narrowed the police's suspects down to two, he was sure he'd done nothing to point the finger of guilt at himself. He was handling it.

Earlier he would have hesitated to ask a woman like Rae Borchard out to lunch; now he wasn't even surprised when she said yes. Rae suggested a Japanese restaurant on First Avenue and said she'd meet him there at twelve-thirty. King killed time until the hour approached; he didn't want to go back to the apartment and face Mimi just yet. The thought struck him that it was one week to the day since Dennis and Gregory had died. He'd survived seven days.

Rae was waiting at the restaurant when he got there. Warren Osterman had filled her in on King's suggestion that they sell the Defense Department on the idea of a bigger gun platform, and she was all for it. Rae had mastered the art of talking and reading a menu at the same time, but King still had to jump back and forth between the two.

The food was good and the talk pleasant, touching as it did on any subject except the police investigation. Rae did drop a hint that the next time he had an idea such as the one for the expanded platform, he should come to her with it. But she did it so gracefully that King wasn't at all sure he'd been reprimanded.

She seemed to be waiting for him to bring up the subject on both their minds, so he did. When a lull appeared in the conversation, he asked, "Aren't you afraid to be having lunch with me? The police think I might be a murderer."

Rae gave him the ghost of a smile. "Warren's convinced it's Mimi."

"Warren was also convinced a rival company was out to kill off our entire design team, and he was wrong about that. But

I'm asking what you think."

She patted her mouth with a napkin before she answered. "I don't think you're a murderer, King. You're not a hunter. It doesn't seem to be your nature to pick out a prey and stalk it. The trouble is, I can't see Mimi killing those two men either. Dirty her hands *murdering* somebody? No. I have to think the police are on the wrong track."

King only half believed her. She wasn't really risking anything, meeting him in a public place like this. They'd been alone together only once, the time she drove him home from the hospital; but he wasn't a suspect then. "Rae," he said quietly, "I want you to tell me how much Mimi has been campaigning for my job. Since Dennis and Gregory died, I mean. Exactly what has she been doing?"

"She hasn't approached me at all. Warren mentioned she'd been after him about it, but he didn't go into detail."

Again, he only half believed her. "You know she's senior partner of SmartSoft now."

Rae stared at him, unblinking. "Yes."

"Let me ask you this. If I'd not gone out that morning and had been killed along with Dennis and Gregory—would you have built a new design team from scratch? Or would Mimi now be in charge of the project?"

She took her time answering. Finally she said, "Mimi would be in charge."

King nodded, as if to say *I thought so*, and let the subject drop. He didn't want to make overt accusations, only to plant suspicion. "Warren seems to have abandoned the idea of a conference here with the Defense Department. You couldn't reach all of them, was that it?"

Once more she took her time, obviously choosing her words carefully. "That's true, but there's a little more involved than that. Unfortunately, there's been a slight change of attitude in Washington. Defense knows that the New York police now believe the killer to be you or Mimi. This has, ah, put a damper on their enthusiasm, you might say."

King's blood turned to ice. "We're going to lose the contract."

"Not necessarily," she said quickly. "If the police arrest one of you soon and we're able to provide a satisfactory replacement, then there's no problem."

"Replacement. I'll bet you already have replacements picked out for both Mimi *and* me."

She didn't even look embarrassed. "We have to be prepared for all contingencies."

He couldn't believe it. "No. Warren wouldn't just dump me like that."

A touch of something that might have been pity appeared on her face. "But it's not Warren's decision to make, don't you see? He's given me full authority over all these new Defense contracts—not just the EM gun platform but all the other projects as well. And I'll tell you honestly, King, that I will jettison anything or anybody that endangers any one of the contracts."

"I see," he said tightly.

"So it really does depend upon how quickly the police act. If they arrest, ah, Mimi . . . before the boys at Defense get really antsy, that is, then we have nothing to worry about. I'll simply call in her replacement and we'll get on with the job."

"And if the police don't make an arrest?"

She spread her hands, said nothing.

King felt as if he'd been hit in the mouth with a baseball bat. No arrest meant he and Mimi both would be out. All along he'd been hoping to create such a cloud of suspicion that the police would never know for certain who was responsible for Dennis's and Gregory's deaths. But obviously that wouldn't do now. He was going to lose the opportunity of a lifetime if the police didn't make an arrest, and he was going to lose it fairly soon. *Oh Mimi, Mimi!* He didn't have much time.

The talk between Rae and him was stiff after that, and they both gave a little sigh of relief when the waiter appeared with the check. Outside, the rain had started again. Rae had brought an umbrella with her, one of the big kind that came all the way down over the shoulders. King had to scrunch down to walk under it with her, but huddling together under an umbrella did a lot to ease the tension between them. He made a bad joke and she laughed, doing her part. Along with what seemed like hundreds of other people, they were trying to get a taxi.

They'd stepped off the curb into the street, both of them waving an arm in a vain attempt to catch a cab driver's attention. A car came barreling down First Avenue, too fast, hitting every puddle and spraying the taxi-hunters with dirty rainwater. "Look out!" Rae cried, and grabbed King's arm.

She caught him by surprise; he was still off balance when the speeding car sloshed him and another man, who knocked against King in his eagerness to get out of the way. King felt himself falling . . . directly into the line of traffic.

A screech tore through the air as the driver of a green van stood on his brake pedal to stop in time. He missed King, but the rear end of the van slewed around on the wet street to bang into the front fender of a Porsche in the next lane. The crash was a real attention-getter; all the cars behind the two vehicles started honking their horns.

Shaken by his close call, King examined himself for damage. Other than a tear in his trousers and a skinned knee, he seemed to be all right. Then the van driver was bending over him, breathing anxiously in his face. "Did I hitcha? Did I hitcha?"

"No, no," King assured him hastily. "You stopped in time."

"Ohhhhh, will you *look* what you did to my cah!" a nasal voice lamented.

The van driver stood up and jerked around to face the owner of the Porsche. "Jesus, buddy, what did you want me to do? Run the guy down?"

Rae held her umbrella over King, her face chalk-white. "My god, King—I almost got you killed. Oh . . . can you get up?" He took the hand she offered and pulled himself creakily to his feet. She looked at his torn trousers and said, "Your knee is bleeding! Oh King—I'm so sorry!" Her face was tight and her voice high; she was more upset by what had happened than King was.

"Don't worry about it, Rae," he said as calmly as he could, "it was just an accident." As King looked at her anguished face, the thought suddenly came to him: *But if it had been Mimi who'd caused it instead of you* . . . Yes. Oh yes. He tried not to smile as the idea took hold.

"Are you sure you're all right?"

All the pedestrians around them were busy telling one another what had just happened, and the chorus of honking horns was growing louder as the traffic backed up behind the two stopped vehicles. The van driver and the owner of the Porsche were engaged in a spirited shouting match. "Let's get out of here," King muttered.

He took Rae's arm and they melted into the crowd. No one noticed when they went down into the first subway stop they came to and made their escape.

Mimi was at the apartment. "What happened to you?" she demanded, staring at King's rain-soaked clothing and the tear in his trousers.

"An accident," he said shortly and headed toward his room. She followed. "What kind of accident?"

King told her what had happened and closed the bedroom door firmly in her face. He cleaned off his scraped knee and put on dry clothing. He glanced in the mirror; one good thing, the bruises on his face were faint now, almost unnoticeable. He flopped down on the bed to think.

If he were the victim of an "accident" that Mimi seemed to have caused, would that be enough for the police to arrest her? It would have to be a near-fatal accident, and there couldn't be any doubt as to Mimi's involvement. How could he arrange that? And he'd need a witness. Marian Larch would be ideal.

Rae Borchard was only partly right about him. Never before in his life had he set out to get someone; but he could learn to be a hunter if that's what it took to survive. He had changed, and he could change even more. In a way he was lucky that the only other suspect was Mimi Hargrove; if it had been someone he liked, such as Gale Fredericks, he wasn't at all sure he could go ahead with it no matter how much he'd changed. But it was Mimi, good old thorn-in-the-side, double-crossing Mimi. Mimi, who wanted his job so badly she could . . . kill for it?

The police were still thinking in terms of deliberate murder, bless their one-track little minds. All right: if they wanted a murderer, he'd give them one. He was damned if he'd see his own life ruined because of two stupid mistakes he'd made. But whatever he was going to do, he'd better do it fast; the people in Washington weren't going to wait forever.

Mimi. He'd better find out if she was thinking of moving to a hotel or not. He found her in the media room, watching two movies. King put on a hearty air and asked, "Neither one interesting enough to hold your full attention?"

Her face was unreadable as she turned down the sound of the one movie she was listening to as well as watching. "I called Michael," she said expressionlessly. "As soon as his ship reaches port, he's catching the next plane here."

Damn her—even less time now. "You're afraid to stay in the apartment with me?"

"Ivan says you won't dare kill me now."

Ivan? "Well, *Marian* says the same about you."

Mimi switched off the two movies and stood up to face him. "King, you're not going to kill me. I'm going to be watching you, every minute. And when Michael gets here, we'll both be watching you. Knowing you, I think you'll give yourself away sooner or later. I'm not going to jail for you."

He didn't like the sound of that. "Give myself away? Is that what you said?"

"Just remember—I'm watching. Don't do *anything* out of the ordinary and you must might get out of this intact." She stared at him, unblinking.

It didn't make sense; if she accepted the police's theory and believed him to be a murderer, why the hell was she still here? Play it out. "If you think the police are going to arrest me for murder, you're wrong. There's no way they can prove I did something I didn't do."

She laughed unpleasantly. "I can't believe how naive you are. Those two detectives can make a case against either of us anytime they feel like it. They can argue we each had motive and we each had opportunity, and neither of us can prove them wrong. Once they get tired of playing these games with us, they can just flip a coin to decide which of us to arrest."

Uh-huh, so that was it; she didn't trust the police to get it right. That meant she was up to no good, that she had something definite in mind. But what? Ask her. "What are you going to do?"

"I'm going to watch you," she replied.

"I see. Well, if you think I won't be keeping an eye on *you*, better think again. I'm not going to be done in by some programmer from California."

Mimi's upper lip lifted. "You're a prince, King," she said without realizing how silly that sounded. "Now we both know where we stand."

They were glaring at each other without speaking when the doorbell rang. And rang again. Finally Mimi broke away and went to answer the door. "Oh no," he heard her groan.

King took his time getting to the entryway, where he saw the two people he fully expected to see. "Sergeants Larch and Malecki. What a surprise."

"We didn't want you to think we were neglecting you," Marian Larch said with unnecessary heartiness.

"Never," King replied somberly.

"We had something to attend to or we woulda been here earlier," Ivan Malecki explained to Mimi, as if she wanted to know.

"Well, Mimi, you can relax," King said sarcastically. "Now you won't have to *watch* me by yourself."

She ignored him, superbly. "What do you want this time, Ivan? I'm not answering any more questions. My lawyer told me not to talk to you at all."

My lawyer, King noted.

"Oh, I thought we'd just sit and talk for a while," the detective answered amiably. "King and my partner have an errand to run."

"We do?" King said.

"We do," Marian answered firmly. "Got a raincoat? It's still pouring down outside."

King looked in the entryway closet. No guest raincoats, but a couple of umbrellas. He took one and asked, "Where are we going?"

"I want you to meet some people."

You don't have to go with her, he told himself. "On second thought, I don't think so. I don't have to go trotting along after you every time you—"

"You can either come with me to meet these people or I take you down to the station and hold you as a material witness. Well? Which is it going to be?"

He glared at her. "Oh, shit. All right. Who are these people?"

"You'll see. Come along." She turned and went out, not looking back to see if he followed.

He followed.

On the street, King folded himself into the passenger seat of the car Marian was driving, a different one from yesterday's. He felt more curiosity than nervousness. A couple of weeks ago, being dragged off to god-knows-where by a police detective would have reduced him to a twittering wreck; but now he simply felt a healthy tenseness, ready to take on whatever it was. The rain was beginning to slack off.

"This morning the reports from your credit card companies came in," Marian said conversationally. "Copies of receipts, like that. We were interested in the ones that were dated after you were mugged. And you know what we found? We found a whole bunch of receipts for that same day."

King had halfway expected this to happen. "A few of them are bound to be mine," he said coolly. "I made some charges right before the muggers took my billfold."

"That's what we figured. But it's the damnedest thing—you know what your muggers used your cards for that day? Food! Not expensive clothes or televisions or high-tech toys, but food. They went down to Fifty-seventh Street and gorged themselves. Isn't that strange?"

King shrugged. "What did they charge after that day?"

"Nothing. Probably keeping the cards out of circulation for a while. But after they mugged you, they evidently spent the rest of the day eating. At least, that's what we thought. My partner and I checked them out—that's what we've been doing today. It was a long shot, at best. Cashiers and waiters don't even look at the customers half the time. But guess what? We found a couple who did."

King's skin began to itch.

Marian went on, "One of them looked at the receipt and said, 'Oh, yeah, that's the dude who's fifteen feet tall—I remember him.' Well, you can imagine our surprise. You said *kids* mugged you, so it was kids we were looking for. But the description we got was of a middle-aged man, kind of messy, and tall. *Extremely* tall. Easy to notice, easy to remember."

He tried to sound casual. "Those are two places I went, obviously."

"Obviously. But what has us puzzled is the time stamps. One receipt says three-forty-five and the other six-oh-five. Hours after you were supposed to have been mugged. Well, here we are."

Here was the Russian Tea Room. King numbly followed her inside. He hadn't even known that the time appeared on credit card receipts; he'd never looked at them that closely. Immediately he recognized the sad-eyed Polish waiter who'd cleaned up some wine King had spilled; King stood there uneasily as the waiter unsmilingly identified him. Then Marian took him to Tony Roma's, where it was the cashier who made the identification. King didn't remember her at all.

The rain had stopped. Marian had parked illegally, but when they got in she made no move to start the car. She looked at King and said, "Want to tell me about it?"

"Obviously I got the time confused." He let a trace of irritation creep into his voice.

"Obviously. You confused high noon with seven o'clock in the evening—a common mistake. All the time you were supposed to be lying unconscious in Central Park, you were down here stuffing your gut. Why did you tell us you were attacked at noon?"

Be friendly, be reasonable. "Marian, I'd just suffered a head injury. Had you forgotten that? I don't really remember what I told the investigating officers. I'm not sure about the times even now."

She cocked an eyebrow at him. "Good answer. It might just play in a courtroom." Abruptly she started the car. "I need a beer."

So did King.

Marian headed back toward the western half of Fifty-seventh, parked illegally again, and led King into a bar called Desmond's. One of the places he'd missed. King felt as if he'd stepped into another era, a time usually thought of as the age of innocence. The old-fashioned wooden bar, the total absence of steel and plastic, the unhurried pace, the quiet. If the barman had been a soda jerk, the scene could have been painted by Norman Rockwell.

They sat at the bar to drink their beers. King watched the barman polishing already gleaming glasses and said a little prayer that Marian Larch would let him off the hook.

She didn't. "There were receipts from ten different restaurants, you know. All the same day. Ten! Why were you eating so much?"

He gave a little laugh, trying to sound mildly embarrassed. "A childhood habit, I'm afraid. I go on eating binges when I'm uptight."

"What were you uptight about?"

"I was about to start on the project that could make me or break me and you want to know what I was uptight about? Come on."

A silence fell. The barman started placing his newly polished glasses on a shelf behind the bar, aligning them just so. Each one separated from its neighbor by the exact same amount of space, each one back from the edge of the shelf the same distance. Marian said, "You couldn't have been mugged before six-thirty, seven o'clock, because you left the last restaurant at five after six. But the time on the first credit card receipt is only a few minutes after noon. What were you doing all morning?"

"Eating. I paid cash until I ran low and then started charging."

"Uh-huh. So you spent the *entire day* eating?"

"Yeah, I guess I did."

"You were so uptight about the project that could make you or break you—your words—that you spent the day eating . . . when you should have been at MechoTech?"

"What?"

"You had a meeting at two o'clock, but you didn't show. Because you were too busy eating?"

"A meeting?" King stalled.

"Rae Borchard says all four of you were expected at two. She'd wanted to reschedule for an hour earlier, but her secretary couldn't get any of you on the phone. The secretary had started calling a little after nine and kept calling all morning."

A picture flashed into King's head: his own hands struggling to hold up the heavy window while Gregory fed his one-footed pigeon, the ringing of the telephone distracting him for one crucial moment, the feeling of helplessless as the window began to slip out of his grasp . . . "Are you sure about the day? I thought the meeting was for the next day, Friday."

The police detective looked at him with disgust. "You didn't show up for that meeting because you knew there wasn't going to be any meeting. And you knew there wasn't going to be any meeting because you knew half the design team was dead. What happened in that apartment?"

"How would I know? I wasn't there!"

"Oh, knock it off, Sauerkraut!" Marian said sharply. "Of course you were there. What happened?" The barman looked up at her tone.

The only word King heard was *Sauerkraut*. That name again—that insulting, degrading name! Now even the goddam New York *Police* Department knew about it. How?

How? "Listen, Marian. The only reason I didn't show up for that meeting is that I thought it was scheduled for the next day. I left the apartment before Dennis and Gregory died. You got that? *Before*."

He might as well not have spoken. "Dennis must have been your primary target. Then you had to kill Gregory because he just happened to be there."

"No, dammit! You couldn't be more wrong. I don't think they were murdered at all."

"Two accidents at the same time? I could buy one, but not two. Was that how it happened? You killed Dennis by accident and then murdered Gregory to get rid of a witness?"

King clenched his teeth. "I . . . have never . . . murdered . . . anyone."

"Then they both *were* accidents? Maybe I should charge you with reckless endangerment and take you in right now. But I don't think so. You knocked the TV set into the bathwater and then for an encore you dropped a window on Gregory Dillard's neck. Or was Gregory first?"

He pushed the empty beer glass away from him. "I'm not going to talk to you anymore."

"Well, that would be a mistake, because Mimi Hargrove's talking her head off. She told my partner that Dennis was trying to sell Keystone out from under you. She said Warren Osterman was going for a merger with both Keystone and SmartSoft, but you told her you'd only recently found out about it. That means Dennis had been negotiating with Osterman behind your back. You found out what was going on, and—*wham!* I got to tell you, King, you're looking good for this one. You killed your partner to stop his betraying you, and then you had to get rid of Gregory Dillard to shut him up."

Wrong wrong wrong wrong wrong! But he said nothing, refusing to be baited.

"Although I have to admit that decapitation by falling window is a rather unusual way of murdering someone," Marian went on. "Gregory must not have known Dennis was dead—no, he couldn't have. He wouldn't have stopped to feed the pigeons otherwise . . . or trusted you to hold the window. But since you were the only other one in the apartment, he'd have known eventually. That's the way it was, right?"

Wrong. King kept his mouth clamped shut.

"Mimi says you and Dennis didn't get along—there was bad feeling between you even before all this talk about a merger. She says you were jealous of his talent and stuck him with managing the business so you could keep all the big projects for yourself. She told Ivan that the real reason you wanted Gale Fredericks for your partner was that Gale wouldn't be the competition that Dennis was."

King clenched his teeth. Mimi was doing her damnedest to make sure the police zeroed in on him. She was doing exactly the same thing to him that he'd been doing to her—only she was doing it better.

"You've got the motive all right, Sauerkraut, no question of that," Marian said conversationally. "And you don't really have an alibi. All the eating as well as the mugging took place hours afterward. Yes, indeed, you're looking good for it."

I have changed, I have changed, King repeated to himself like an incantation. *I will not rise to the bait. I will keep my mouth shut and I will ride this out.*

Marian Larch kept after him, but eventually she had to accept the fact that he just wasn't going to talk anymore. Grumpily she paid for their beers and drove him home.

In the car, he broke his silence once. "How did you know about that name Sauerkraut?" he asked.

"Warren Osterman told me. When he was trying to convince me that you were too clumsy to carry out a successful double murder."

She let him out at the apartment building. He waited in the foyer until he saw her drive away and then slipped back out again. There were things he had to do, and little time in which to do them.

* 12 *

The rain had slackened into a soft drizzle; King turned up his jacket collar and wondered where he'd left the umbrella. Hell of a time to go shopping. King let loose a sigh; it would be the simplest thing in the world for him to construct a small robot and use it to cause an "accident". A remote-controlled toy car would be the easiest way to start; any electronics store could supply the capacitors and resistors and photocells and other parts he'd need to modify it. The right-sized circuit boards might be a little harder to find, but they'd be available somewhere.

However—and it was a very big however—this little accident was supposed to pass as one that *Mimi* had rigged; would it be that easy for her to build a robot, even a simple one, by herself? Not very likely. That wasn't her area of expertise; it was his. If King used a robot, any kind of robot, he might as well sign his name. No one would be fooled.

So robots were out, alas. What would Mimi do, if she truly were out to kill him? She'd probably go for something that could be made to look like a domestic accident, something that could reasonably be expected to happen in the apartment—such as a falling window, or an appliance in the bathwater. But all the windows in the second apartment opened outward, not up. And fortunately, or unfortunately, King took showers instead of baths. Mimi wouldn't know that, though, unless she made a habit of peeking through keyholes. *Think like Mimi:* Does King Sarcowicz take showers or baths? Oh dear, I don't know.

No bathroom accident, then. And no bedroom accident, either, simply because King couldn't figure out a way to make it work. Therefore: the media room. That was the place.

He needed tools, wire, clamps, and the like. A couple of remote controls—one to use and one to plant in Mimi's room. But that afternoon's trip to Fifty-seventh Street with Marian Larch had reinforced a lesson King first learned years ago: strangers remembered him. Including, presumably, clerks in hardware and electronic stores. So he loitered in front of a big hardware store on Forty-second Street until a boy of high-school age came by; King offered him twenty dollars to go into the store and fill an order for him. The kid wanted thirty but settled for twenty-five; fifteen minutes later King had what he needed.

The drizzling rain had stopped. The wet streets cast up reflections of hundreds of neon lights, giving a *noir*ish look to the oncoming night that well suited King's mood. He repeated the procedure he'd used at the hardware store at two different electronics shops. Loaded down, he found himself wishing he'd thought to bring along his new briefcase to carry some of his supplies. No sooner had he thought that than he spied a bag lady hauling three full shopping bags along the street. "I'll give you ten dollars for one of those bags," he said to her.

She looked at him suspiciously. "It's worth fifty."

They agreed on fifteen. The old woman dumped out the contents of one of the bags right there on the sidewalk—men's shoes, a couple of sweaters and a flowered skirt, a plastic vanity mirror, a package of cocktail napkins, an AT&T 800-number directory, two *Blake's 7* buttons, one wool glove. The bag was old and well worn, but it held all of King's packages. He left the bag lady redistributing her possessions between her other two shopping bags.

King was hungry, but it was turning dark and there was no time for a restaurant; street food would have to do. He bought a gyro and ate the juicy, dripping sandwich as he looked around for a taxi, all of which seemed to be headed in the wrong direction. He started walking.

His route took him past a Radio Shack on Broadway, and the window display made him pause. Red Racer, with a roll cage, $9.95. A radio-controlled toy car that could be adapted into an autonomous robot. A soldering iron and the right parts . . . the robot would need only the simplest of functions to do the job. *Search, avoid,* possibly *follow*—

No. No robots. King plowed on homeward.

The rain was just starting up again by the time he reached the apartment. One of the security guards in the lobby told him his lady friend was waiting for him upstairs. King groaned; evidently Marian Larch didn't have anything to do with her life except hassle him.

But it wasn't the police detective who was waiting; it was Gale Fredericks. And she looked absolutely miserable. "Gale! What's wrong? What are you doing here?"

"I had to talk to you . . . in person. Is this a good time?"

"Sure. Just let me dump this stuff in my room." He did so and came back to where Gale was nervously pacing in the living room. "Where's Mimi?"

"In the office room. She won't come out—she talked to me through the door. King, what's going on?"

He grimaced. "Mimi thinks I'm the murderer the police are looking for. Or at least she's pretending she does."

Gale was astonished. "But . . . but that's absurd! How could you . . . besides, if she really thinks you're a murderer, why is she still here in the apartment?"

"That's the part I haven't figured out." There was an awkward pause. "Gale, I'm always glad to see you, but what are you doing here? Is something wrong in Pittsburgh?"

"No, everything is fine." She took a deep breath and plunged in. "What's wrong is me. I can't do it, King. I just can't do it."

King felt a ringing in his ears. "Oh, Gale!"

"I know I told you I would, and I even got caught up in the excitement of the design . . . I shouldn't have let that happen. I should never have let myself be seduced by the challenge."

"Gale—"

"Don't, King. Even before my plane landed in Pittsburgh Sunday, every cell in my body was shrieking *No!* I've spent the last few days trying to talk myself into it, into keeping my word—but it's impossible. I simply cannot contribute to a killing machine. I can't do it."

"You don't have to work on the weapons," King said desperately. "I'll put you in charge of locomotion. *You* can solve the problem of where to put the extra wheels and legs and—"

"Oh, King, you don't really think that makes a difference? I'd still be helping build a war machine." She smiled wanly. "Besides, I know how much you want to do the locomotion yourself. I appreciate the offer, but the answer is still no."

King argued. He cajoled. He tried sophistry and emotional backmail. He appealed to her professionalism, to her ambition, to her loyalty to him. Then he made the mistake of slipping into a threat; he told her that the kind of partner he was looking for was one who wouldn't let him down, one who wouldn't let her personal convictions interfere with business.

"I thought it might come to that," Gale said wryly, "so I'm going to save you the trouble of making that decision. I can't stay on at Keystone now. You didn't make the partnership contingent on my working on the gun platform . . . but it was lurking there beneath the surface all the same, wasn't it? But partnership or no partnership, I just can't stay with a company that accepts Defense contracts. I don't want to have anything at all to do with weapons."

"Gale, you've tossed me a curve, I'm saying things I don't mean—of course I want you to stay, and as my partner. I never—"

She held up a hand to stop him. "Gun people never really understand how *repulsive* their weapons are to non-gun people, do they? Guns can have a hypnotic effect, you know. King, you're no warmonger, but you've gotten so caught up in the lure of the technology that you've blocked everything else out." She dropped her hand in a gesture of hopelessness. "Oh, what's the use. You think I'm a kook and I think you're sick. We'll never agree."

King stared at her icily. "You think I'm sick."

"If you can talk yourself out of thinking about the people you'll be helping to kill—yes, I'd say that's sick." She hesitated. "King, I'm sorry. I didn't know it would end on such an ugly note. I came here to say goodbye. Shake hands?"

He turned his back on her outstretched hand. She spoke his name, but said nothing more when he didn't answer. After a few moments he heard her leave.

To fight against drowning in disappointment, King tried to talk to Mimi. But the door to the office was locked. Mimi yelled through the door for him to go away and leave her alone.

He'd lost Gale. Lost her permanently—she wouldn't even be working with him anymore. Damn the woman! How could she do it? He'd offered her half his business; *nobody* turned down an offer like that just to maintain some self-flattering, high-minded moral posture. There had to be some other reason. One of his competitors must have made her a better offer; that was it. She'd turn up as European Director of Rhobotics International or some big outfit like that. Or maybe Warren Osterman had offered to make her heir apparent instead of

Rae Borchard—no, that was ridiculous. King was finding it harder and harder to trust anybody.

But Gale was gone, and that was that. The old King would have sat around and moped about his loss, mooning over what might have been and feeling sorry for himself. But the new King had work to do.

Get to it. His plan was to rig a short in the media room's control unit touch screen, just enough to make the unit hiss and spark and give a mild shock to whoever was handling the unit. Mimi knew about wiring; an attempt to electrocute him would be more in keeping with her abilities than the use of a homemade robot. The short would be "detonated" by a remote control he'd carry in a jacket pocket and then dispose of as soon thereafter as possible; a second remote keyed to the same frequency would then be discovered in Mimi's room.

He took care of that part first, while Mimi was keeping herself locked in the office. What was she doing in there? Why hadn't she locked herself into her bedroom if she was just trying to avoid him? He slipped into her room and looked around. Under the mattress? Too obvious. He used a dime to loosen the screws in a ventilator grid and pushed the remote control unit into the vent. That should do it.

The media room door had a lock on it too and King used it; he didn't want Mimi walking in on him while he had the control unit open. He got to work. He wanted to run a test when he finished, so that meant he'd have to wire up his dummy weapon twice. And it had to be done tonight; for all he knew, Mimi's husband could show up as soon as tomorrow.

King was counting on Marian Larch's putting in an early appearance the next day; he'd be watching a movie when she arrived, so he could say *Come on into the media room, I left a movie running.* If he could think of a way to get her to use the control unit, that would be good. But if not, he'd do it himself. All she had to do was witness what was supposed to be Mimi's unsuccessful attempt on his life. Then he'd open up the unit, examine the wiring, and exclaim in a tone of great wonder that the unit appeared to have been booby-trapped. He'd mention it was probably set off by remote control and leave it to the already suspicious detective to do the rest.

Sergeant Larch wouldn't simply take his word for it about the booby trap; they'd have to wait for the police's expert to examine it. But that plus the remote control concealed in Mimi's ventilator shaft would surely be enough for the police to charge her with attempted murder. And even though they could never prove she had anything to do with the deaths of Dennis Cox and Gregory Dillard, they'd be satisfied that she was guilty and investigate no further. King would hand them their "murderer" gift-wrapped, and then they'd have to leave him alone.

And he would have Mimi Hargrove out of his hair as well.

It wouldn't go as smoothly as all that, of course; things never did. He'd have to keep on his toes, be ready to bounce in any direction. *Stay loose.* He'd watch Marian Larch closely, take his cues from her.

Then it was time for the test. King felt a little nervous about sending even a mild jolt of electricity through his body, but it had to be done. He steeled himself and pressed the button. The control unit accommodatingly popped and sparked, King's body twitched from the electric shock—and all the lights went out.

Damn. That was something he hadn't counted on, shorting out the apartment lights. But as he floundered in the dark toward the door, he thought maybe that wasn't such a bad thing; it would add a nice theatrical touch. But right then he had to get the lights back on.

Mimi was yelling from behind her locked door. "It won't work, King—I'm not coming out!"

Mimi Hargrove, the center of the universe. "I don't give a damn whether you come out or not," King yelled back. "Do you know where there's a flashlight?"

A pause. "Maybe in the kitchen."

The switch box must be inside a closet, most likely the one in the entryway; King was closer to there than to the kitchen. He felt his way through the darkened apartment, hitting his shins and swearing. He thought he remembered seeing a bowl of matches bearing the MechoTech logo somewhere, but he'd never find it in the dark. Finally he reached the entryway and located the switch box in an inside closet wall. He fumbled the switch box door open and ran his fingers over the circuit breakers, locating one large one at the top: the master switch. King pressed it; the lights came on. Now everything digital in the apartment would have to be reset.

He went to the office door and banged on it once with his fist. "All right?"

"All right," Mimi's voice said.

Back to the media room. King replaced the burned-out wires in the video control unit and rigged his false weapon the exact way he'd done it the first time. The lights flickered once while he was working but didn't go out. *The wiring in this whole apartment needs to be checked*, he thought absently. Then he slipped a videocassette into one of the VCRs and played a little of it, just enough to make sure his electronic equivalent of a smoke bomb didn't interfere with the normal operation of the equipment. He left the cassette in the player, ready for viewing tomorrow morning when Marian Larch would be there to act as his eyewitness. Then he gathered up his tools and leftover wires and parts, tied them all together, and tossed the bundle down the apartment's trash-disposal chute.

Everything was ready.

It was only ten o'clock, but King's body was telling him to go to bed. He passed the office door without calling out goodnight to Mimi and locked himself into his bedroom. A quick shower made him even more conscious of the fatigue that had been creeping up on him for some time now; it had been an event-filled day. King reset the clock radio by his bed and crawled under the comforter, relishing its soft warmth.

He thought briefly of Gale Fredericks. He'd lost her, irrevocably. He'd lost both the people he'd worked most closely with, but Dennis Cox would leave no unfillable gap in his life. Gale, however, had been more than a co-worker; she was the only woman he'd really wanted, for a long time. And now she was gone. She'd run out on him when he needed her the most; that must surely be the ugliest kind of betrayal there was. King wondered what he had ever seen in her.

He was calm. Sleep came easily.

The clock radio woke him early the next morning; he didn't know what time the police would show up and he didn't want to rush. He stared at his face in the bathroom mirror. The bruises were almost gone.

He made coffee and ate a bowl of cereal; there was no sign of Mimi. When he'd finished breakfast, he looked in her room. The bed was made. She must have gotten an even earlier start than he did or else the bed hadn't been slept in. Was she *sleeping* in the office? How uncomfortable.

King went into the media room and started the movie. It was a spy thriller he'd already seen, so he let it run as he wandered restlessly around the apartment. He went out on the living room balcony and glanced down at the street, twenty-two stories away, trying to spot a car pulling up to the front of the building. *Come on, Sergeant Larch.*

Mimi's behavior was peculiar, to say the least; King didn't even know whether she was in the apartment or not. Maybe she didn't think he was the killer at all; it could be that was just a defensive posture she'd decided it would be smart to adopt. So what was she up to? When he couldn't stand it any longer, he went to the office door and knocked. "Mimi!" he called. "Are you in there?"

There was no answer. He tried the knob; the door was still locked. "Come on, Mimi, answer me! I know you're there."

He stood listening for some sound from behind the locked door. The only noise in the apartment came from the soundtrack of the movie he'd left playing in the media room; from all the racket it was making, the bad guys must be blowing something up. King began to get uneasy. Mimi had spoken to him through the door last night—why wouldn't she answer now? Was this some sort of trap she'd set for him?

He examined the doorknob. It was the kind with a small insert hole in the middle, a safety precaution for rescuing small children who accidentally locked themselves into bathrooms and the like. All he needed was something small enough to fit into the hole and he'd have the door open in no time. King straightened up and thought; among the tools he'd tossed the night before was a tiny screwdriver that would have done the job admirably, but he wasn't about to go down to the basement and rummage through the trash looking for it.

A wire coat hanger. But every closet he looked in had only wooden and plastic hangers. What else would fit in the hole? A knitting needle. An ice pick? Too big. A meat skewer, one of the thin ones used for kabobs. A quick search through the kitchen drawers turned up a dozen metal skewers of just the right size.

King took one and hurried back to the office. He poked the skewer into the hole and heard the lock click open. He opened the door cautiously, in case Mimi was standing there ready to brain him with some conveniently heavy object.

She wasn't. In fact, she wasn't standing at all; she was slumped over the conference table as if asleep. But King didn't have to go into the room to know she wasn't asleep. Even from the doorway he could tell that of all the senseless things that had been happening, the most senseless had now taken place. Mimi was dead.

Quietly he closed the door on the sight and leaned his forehead against the panel, his heart pounding and his pulse racing. First Gregory. Then Dennis. And now . . . Mimi. He himself was the sole survivor of that ill-fated design team; and if there was any one thing in the world that would convince the police that King Sarcowicz was a bloodthirsty killer who ought to be locked away for ten thousand years, this was it. Mimi was dead.

Mimi was dead!

How? When? How? King fought down the beginnings of panic and tried to think. The other time this had happened, he'd bolted; but the new King would have to react more rationally if he was going to have any chance of getting out of this. First things first. Go inside, try to figure out what happened. *Then* decide what to do.

He opened the door again and forced himself to go up to where Mimi lay slumped over the table. Her lips were blue and her body was rigid; she'd been dead for hours. One hand still gripped a soldering iron tightly. A soldering iron? Only then did King notice that the tabletop was littered with tiny electronic parts. Slowly he walked around the table, taking inventory.

Capacitors. Switching diodes. Transistors. Trim pots. Resistors. Toggle switches. NAND gates. Infrared proximity sensors. IC sockets. Circuitry boards. And in the middle of it all, a radio-controlled toy car.

King's mouth fell open. "Why, you bitch!" he said aloud.

She'd been building a robot. A robot! The one thing that the police would leap on as carrying King's signature. Mimi Hargrove had been planning the same thing he'd been planning, to stage a fake accident that would bear all the earmarks of having been engineered by the *other* suspect. She was manufacturing evidence to incriminate him.

King sank down in a chair across the table from Mimi's body. He knew she hadn't trusted the police to solve the case on their own, but it never occurred to him that she'd go this far to make sure *she* was not the one they arrested. But that's what she'd been doing; and that's why she'd locked herself into this room—she needed the big table to work on. Morbidly curious, King examined the work she'd completed. Goddam. She was getting it right.

His stomach did a flipflop as he realized what a close call he'd had. If she'd finished . . . if she'd finished, his own carefully staged "accident" wouldn't convince anybody of anything. At best, the two accidents would cancel each other out and the police would remain equally suspicious of both of them. He stared up at the chandelier that had been burning all night and wondered how Mimi had been planning to work it. She could have used the robot to trip herself and cause a bad fall, and then she'd have just handed the toy car to the police.

No, that was too vague, too clumsy. Idly he picked up a pack of adhesive strips from the table. What did she need adhesive strips for? *Holds up to 25 pounds,* the package lettering declared. King thought about that. If Mimi had fitted the adhesive strips around the wheels of the toy car, then the robot might possibly have been able to climb walls. Or . . . the side of a bathtub? She could have filled the tub with water and simply tossed the robot car in; since one of their team had already died that way, that would add a nice note of consistency. Then Mimi would have told the police that she'd seen the robot coming and was able to get out of the tub in time. The toy car would have to be a real, functioning robot for her story to hold up; so she'd been building the one prop her little drama required when she'd died.

Pretty good, Mimi. King raised an eyebrow at her corpse in silent salute. And to think how narrowly he'd escaped all that. If she hadn't died just when she did, before finishing . . . but how did that happen? *Why* did she die, what killed her?

King went over to take a closer look at the body. Mimi had died while working on some soldering; that much was clear. He peered at the soldering iron she was gripping with such intensity, but could see nothing wrong there. His eyes traveled down the soldering iron's cable—and there it was: a big hole in the top side of the cable, with burn marks around the edges. The cable's casing had been seared away and the wires exposed, now fused and blackened. Mimi had electrocuted herself.

God god in heaven, how could that have happened? Obviously she'd put the soldering iron down right on the cable and burned the protective casing away. But didn't she *see* what she was doing? Mimi was not a careless woman, she didn't make dumb mistakes—

Oh. Oh no. She *didn't* see what she was doing. And the reason she didn't see was that the lights were out. She'd put the iron down in the dark, and when she picked it up again after the lights came back on . . .

"*It's not my fault!*" King brayed, shocked and horrified. How was he to know his puny little booby trap would short-circuit the apartment's entire lighting system? And how was he to know Mimi was in here fucking around with a soldering iron? If she hadn't been so busy trying to incriminate *him*, she'd be alive right now! It was her own doing, she'd brought it on herself, if she'd just left it to the police and not meddled . . .

King sank to the floor beside Mimi's chair and buried his face in his hands. Oh god. God. He'd done it again.

After a while he began to feel an irresistible desire to giggle. *Don't mess with me, man—I'll "accident" you to death!* Mimi's last words had been "All right"—in response to his query after he got the lights back on. *Then* she was all right. Later, he'd passed the office door without saying goodnight. She wouldn't have answered even if he had spoken. He remembered the lights flickering while he was working on his own booby trap; that must have been when it happened. His giggle climbed higher and then broke off sharply, as King struggled to get a grip on himself. This was no time to revert to the old King, not with . . . he jerked himself up to his feet. He'd just remembered the police; they, or she, could be on the way right now. Get moving.

What to do? He couldn't be found in the apartment with Mimi's body. And he couldn't just leave and claim to know nothing about it, the way he'd done last time; that hadn't worked too well then and it sure as hell wouldn't work now. So the logical thing was to get rid of the body; if Mimi Hargrove simply disappeared from the face of the earth, they couldn't blame him for that, could they?

But how? How do you dispose of a body with the police watching you and security guards checking off your name every time you go in and out of the building? King still had enough composure left to realize that was too big a problem to solve in the time he had left before Marian Larch put in her daily appearance. So the only thing to do was hide the body for now and figure out how to dispose of it later. He'd tell Marian that Mimi had gone out earlier and didn't say when she'd be back . . . yes, that would do.

He'd hide Mimi in her bedroom closet; Marian Larch would have no reason to go poking around in there. Or better still, in the closet in the unused bedroom. The first thing he did was unplug the soldering iron. Then he braced himself for something he'd been dreading: he had to touch Mimi. He tried to work the soldering iron free of the death grip Mimi had on it but couldn't manage it, and he couldn't bring himself to break her fingers to pry it loose. Didn't matter; just leave it there.

Fighting down a feeling of nausea, King grasped Mimi's body around the waist and lifted her out of her chair—and got an unpleasant shock. Mimi had stiffened into her seated, slumped-over posture, a posture the body maintained even as King lifted her up. *This is grotesque,* he thought, struggling to get a better grip on the nearly folded-double corpse. He almost dropped her, put off as he was by the bizarreness of what he was doing. He used one foot to push the door open a little wider, and after much maneuvering succeeded in getting Mimi's body out into the hallway.

Where he froze. Because from the direction of the apartment's entryway came the sound of voices. He heard a clank of buckets, a woman's laugh, and the noise a vacuum cleaner makes when it starts up. The cleaning crew! It was the goddam cleaning crew! King was paralyzed by the racket they were making, standing there as stiff and unbending as the burden he carried.

"Thanks for letting us in," said a familiar voice.

And then Marian Larch and Ivan Melecki were at the other end of the hallway, staring at him in shock, horror, and just plain disgust. No one said anything, no one moved; the sound of the vacuum cleaner roared in the background. Sergeant Malecki was the first to find his voice. "Put her down," he said tightly.

Slowly King lowered Mimi's body to the floor. Then he stepped back as the two detectives rushed forward.

"Rigor's well advanced," Marian Larch murmured, bending over the body. "She must have died during the night. Ivan . . . ?"

"I'll call it in," he said. "And I'll get rid of those cleaning people." He headed toward the living room.

Marian straightened up and looked King in the eye. "You just couldn't let it go, could you? You just had to get rid of this one last obstacle, didn't you? Whatever made you think you could get away with it? Maybe we can't nail you for the first two—but this time we've got you dead to rights, buddy! You have the right to remain silent—"

"In case you're interested," King said tiredly, "I didn't kill Mimi. She electrocuted herself."

"Oh? You're telling me this is a suicide?"

"Of course it's not a suicide! It was an accident. Look at the soldering iron cable." He explained about the lights going out the night before.

"Uh-huh." Utter disbelief. But she examined the cable; King could hear the vacuum cleaner noise die out as the cleaning crew packed up its things to leave. The detective said, "So it was all an unfortunate accident which you, once again, had nothing to do with. *Why were you moving her body?*"

King twitched. "I was going to hide it until I could figure out what to do. I knew you'd jump to conclusions, you'd think I did it. And you did!" King was starting to feel indignant. "You're so eager to catch a murderer, you can't *wait* to arrest me! Don't you understand? *There is no murderer.* There's been no *murder.*"

"No murder, just three convenient accidents." The distaste on Marian Larch's face spoke volumes. "What was Mimi Hargrove doing with a soldering iron?"

King gestured toward the office with his head. "I'll show you." They went inside, where King pointed toward the table. "She was building a robot."

Marian slowly examined the tabletop without touching anything. "That's a toy, that car."

"It can be adapted into a robot."

"But you're the robot-builder here. What did you do, talk her into helping you and then rig it to electrocute her?"

"No!"

"She wouldn't have been working on a robot if it weren't for you. Or maybe she wasn't working on it at all. Why should I believe anything you tell me?"

She wouldn't have been working on a robot, the words rang in his head, *if it weren't for you.* "This was Mimi's doing. You can see—"

"You know what I think?" Marian asked rhetorically. "I think you were building a robot to go after Mimi and she caught you at it. Then you electrocuted her somehow, and staged all this to make it look as if *she* were the one building the robot. You burned a place in the cable and put the soldering iron in her hand. Then you waited until her body had time to stiffen so we'd find her gripping the soldering iron. But you waited too long."

"That's crazy!" King cried. "If I did all that, why would I want to hide the body?"

"I don't know—second thoughts, maybe? But I do know this is no simple accident, and that you're involved in what happened here."

King was thinking what had happened there was at least half Mimi's fault. But: *She wouldn't have been working on a robot if it weren't for you.* "You really think I'm stupid enough to murder Mimi?"

Marian Larch hesitated. "It would be a stupid thing to do, true—since you knew you were already under suspicion. But if all three of these deaths *were* accidents, they were accidents you caused. You and I both know you're responsible." Her body was starting to slump, as if she were depressed.

What the hell did she have to be depressed about? "I know you think I'm a clumsy lout—and at one time I was. But I've changed, Marian. I'm a different person now."

"So what? It doesn't alter the fact that *we caught you with the body, King.* Hands on the wall."

"What?"

"Put your hands against the wall and spread your feet. You're under arrest."

"Oh, for—haven't you been listening?"

"I'm not going to tell you again."

Disgusted, King did as she ordered and Marian patted him down. "You think I'm carrying guns and knives? Or maybe a bomb?"

She felt something in his jacket pocket. She reached in and took out the remote control. "What's this do?" she asked—and pressed the button.

From another part of the apartment came an unexpected and loud "YOW!" The voice was male, startled, and indignant. The chandelier in the office went out.

Marian stepped to the doorway. "Ivan?" she called. "What's the matter?"

"Bad shock!" Ivan called back. He came into the hallway shaking his right hand. "I went into the media room to turn off a movie and the damned thing near electrocuted me!"

Marian looked at the remote control in her hand and her eyes grew wide. She turned her head slowly toward King. "And still it goes on! Are you crazy, man?" She stepped toward him. "What was this? A back-up plan? Or is this how you got Mimi? You could have killed my partner!" Ivan followed her into the office, astonished at her words.

"No!" King hastened to say. "He was in no danger. Look at him—he's not hurt!"

"No thanks to you. What went wrong? Didn't you wire it up right?"

Ivan took the remote control from Marian's hand. "This is what did it?"

"Yep, that's it. King—what else have you got rigged in this place? Now do we add assault on a police officer to the charges?"

Sweating, King blurted, "You pushed the button!"

She looked disgusted. "Then we'll make it reckless endangerment," she snapped. "You ought to be locked away forever, someplace where you can't go on hurting people!"

"Did you read him his rights?" Ivan asked.

She thought back. "No."

Ivan took care of it. "Hands behind your back," he instructed King.

King stared at Marian while her partner handcuffed him. "This isn't fair!" he protested. "I never wanted to hurt anyone! I'm not a murderer! I didn't want anyone to die!"

Marian looked at him with distaste. "And because your intentions are pure, you shouldn't be held accountable for what you do? That's not the way it works, Sauerkraut. *You caused three deaths.*" She paused. "Maybe you can convince a jury they were accidents, but don't hold your breath. The charge is first-degree murder. This was planned. My advice is to start telling the truth."

They were going to do it; they were actually going to put him in prison! King looked from one detective to the other, but found no sympathy in either face. They were going to make him pay—he'd spend the rest of his life paying. And for what? For a few clumsy mistakes.

"But I've *changed*," he whined.

WITHDRAWN